# FBI Code Name:
# SEACATCH

## *Secrets of Old Baldy*

*To "mo", a wonderful P.T., with much appreciation*

A SPECIAL AGENT DEL DICKERSON NOVEL

*Best wishes*
## Jim Healy

*Jim Healy*

Published by Jimbay Books
©2018 Jim Healy

All rights reserved. No portion of this book may be reproduced, stored in a retrieval system, or transmitted in any form or by any means - electronic, mechanical, photo - copy, recording, scanning or other - except for brief quotations in critical reviews or articles, without prior permission of the author.

Book Cover Design by Sarah Hasty Williams
Artwork by Sarah Hasty Williams
*The Bald Head Island Historical Portfolio of Paintings* © Sarah Hasty Williams 2000 - *The Old Boathouse, Old Baldy, Captain Charlie's Station, Captain Charlies Porch, Deep Peace,* and *Sunrise on South Beach* are also © Sarah Hasty Williams, all rights reserved.

ISBN - 9780990495284

Disclaimer: **FBI Code Name: SEACATCH,** *Secrets of Old Baldy*, is a work of fiction, based on a wide variety of characters encountered during the author's FBI career. Any resemblance to actual persons, living or deceased, is coincidental and unintentional, and merely reflects the author's imagination.

# The Story

North Carolina's iconic "Old Baldy" lighthouse on magical Bald Head Island becomes the unlikely center of unpredictable FBI agent Del Dickerson's latest escapade after he stumbles into a major drug smuggling operation, is knocked unconscious and dumped into the Atlantic Ocean. With near-miraculous luck, he survives to wash up on the remote island. Suffering from temporary amnesia, Del is initially unable to help his frantic searchers who unexpectedly learn of a multi-million dollar cocaine shipment headed to the U.S East coast from Colombia on a Russian-built submarine.

Escalating action erupts during a Memorial Day fire works display when the drug sub surfaces near Carolina Beach. A Coast Guard helicopter is shot down, and gun battles wage between escaping smugglers, Customs vessels, and Navy boats during hot pursuit that abruptly ends on hidden shoals. A shadowy mastermind is identified, and a high-speed chase over murky marshes concludes with alligators feasting on fleeing culprits. Dramatic action explodes in a climatic encounter in the island's historic lighthouse, aided by a 100-pound black Labrador.

Colorful male and female personalities abound, and enticing romances flourish in non-stop action that sees Del emerge battered but intact, finding comfort in the arms of his exotic Amerasian fiancée, Anna Chen. Old Baldy survives another violent hurricane, and its intriguing secrets linger as Del launches a tenacious hunt for an elusive drug dealer just added to the FBI's Ten Most Wanted Fugitive's list. FBI Code Name SEACATCH, Secrets of Old Baldy, is a guaranteed wild read!

# DEDICATION

This book is dedicated to the Patriots who defend us all—the men and women of law enforcement, the military, and the first responders everywhere. Without their selfless sacrifice, none of us would have the precious freedoms we enjoy. The heroes who have paid the ultimate price on our behalf vividly remind us that Freedom Is Not Free. God Bless you all.

Jim Healy, Author

# ACKNOWLEDGMENTS

Heartfelt appreciation is again extended to two incomparable ladies who have labored heroically to bring this story forward—Sandy Robinette and Jacki Byrtus, my priceless editorial review and transcription team. Their hair-pulling corrections of the author's misdirections are saint-like blessings.

An exceptional group of friends and family members have likewise contributed their personal expertise to enrich the plot, too many to individually accord due credit, but representative of several mentioned in no logical order.

Special recognition is due Sarah Hasty Williams, the gifted artist whose striking sketch of Old Baldy graces the cover, supplemented by some of her other inspired sketches of Bald Head Island landmarks.

If you identify Mary Ellen Crocker, Jaimee Field, and Margaret Chapman as resembling an intrepid trio of Bald Head Island ladies, you have earned a gold-plated detective's badge. Congratulations!

Deep appreciation also goes to a group of distinguished friends such as retired Customs official Chuck Brisbin, Vietnam- era helicopter pilot Larry Torrence, valued legal advisor Lee Quick, and ace reviewer Larry Zito.

Warm thanks, too, to the exceptional public servants of Bald Head Island who graciously shared their affection for their magical place, specifically Chief of Police Carl Pearson, Captain Paul Swanson, and Village Clerk, Daralyn Spivey, who richly contributed to the story. Their courtesies to me and my research assistant, Patrick Healy, are deeply appreciated, and I trust they will enjoy their altered personalities. Editorial license be praised!

My gratitude to the family favorite Labrador, Casper, inspiration for the intrepid Rambo, will be demonstrated with a big bag of doggie biscuits.

Finally, thanks to my faithful readers whose allegiance to Del Dickerson and his shenanigans makes this worthwhile.

# Chapter One

<u>CAROLINA BEACH, NORTH CAROLINA</u>

"Ya think he's dead, Rufus?"

"Dunno, Beau, ya hit him pretty hard with that beer bottle."

"But it was Bud Light."

"Filled bottles just as heavy. He dropped like a rock. Ain't moving."

"Looks like he's breathing though. Ya can see that crappy yellow T-shirt moving up and down. Wonder what that big black Y stands for?"

"Who knows, but we gotta get rid of him. He shouldn't have busted into the back room while we was counting the packages."

"Yeah, no respect for the Private sign on the door—right next to the nutty signs Captain Bill installed—Buoys and Gulls."

"Everyone gets confused, Rufus. Heh, heh, I once walked in on Milly Gilmore doing her business. Ya know she's not a real blonde?"

"Hell, every guy in town knows that, Beau."

"Anyway, the guy shouldn't have been snooping, then asking what was in the baggies. Now I have to solve another one of your problems, and get rid of his body."

"My problem! You was here, too. We're both in big trouble with the boss if he finds out. He don't like trouble."

"We gotta think, Beau."

Minutes passed while Rufus Reynolds stroked the

stubble on his weathered, forty-some year-old skin.

"I got it," he finally said, snapping his fingers. "We put him in one of them fish sacks in the corner, and as soon as it gets dark we hustle him out the back door, haul him in your old van to the boat, motor out a few miles and dump him over. Problem solved!"

Beau Chamberlin looked at his cousin with admiration.

"You're a genius, Rufus."

"Guess someone in the family has to have brains," the red-haired fisherman replied with a self-congratulatory smile.

"But not a very good counter," Chamberlin retorted.

"Ya put more packages on your pile—supposed to be equal shares, ya know."

"Oh, sorry. I sure don't want to cheat my favorite cousin."

"Your only cousin, Chamberlin clarified."

"Right. Now let's get busy. The boss will be expecting delivery of this shipment fresh off the boat."

"He's sure one smart dude, Rufus. Imagine, bringing it in on a submarine!"

\* \* \*

Sprawled immobile on the weathered wooden back-room floor of Captain Bill's Sea Shack was faintly breathing FBI Special Agent Del Dickerson.

## Chapter Two

"Want a refill?" the jovial bartender asked Kevin Ryan, perched on a restaurant barstool and displaying a concerned expression as he awaited the overdue arrival of his fishing partner. The early morning ocean excursion had been productive, their bountiful catch currently being processed and iced for the trip home.

"Might as well while I'm waiting, Bunny," Ryan replied, reading the nameplate projecting pertly from the attractive woman's snug Hooter's-style T-shirt.

"Stood up?" Bunny asked with an understanding smile. "I wouldn't do it to a good-looking guy like you. Dumb blonde?"

Ryan grinned and shook his head. "No, dumb guy perhaps, who has an uncanny knack for getting into trouble."

"Your date's a guy? You, ah..., don't look like the guy-guy type."

Ryan laughed. "No, we're what people used to think normal."

"Didn't think so," Bunny said, unleashing a bright smile. "I've seen the slogan on your T-shirt before, The Only Easy Day Was Yesterday. Navy Seal?"

"Former," Ryan replied.

"Thanks for your service. Love you guys. What do you do now?"

"My buddy and I work for the government. We had a couple of days off, which brought us down for the good fishing. We were supposed to meet here for dinner."

"Our restaurant and bar is the best in town. Good

food and booze. When and where did you last see your friend?"

"Late this afternoon. We were having a beer at Captain Bill's Sea Shack. He was finishing his when I left for my motel room to freshen up."

Bunny frowned. "Captain Bill's has a bad rep. Some rough characters hang out there."

"I called there," Ryan said, "No one remembered seeing either of us."

"It's that kind of place," Bunny murmured. "Have you checked around? Town's not that big. Where was he staying?"

Ryan winced. "I don't know. He came in late last night, and never mentioned where he was staying, except it wasn't my place."

"Maybe he got a better offer."

"Doubt it. He's straight arrow, and pretty reliable. Besides, he couldn't go far. I've got most of his gear in my trunk, including his cell phone."

"What's he do?" Bunny asked.

"Like I said, he works for the government. He's an FBI agent."

Bunny's eyebrows raised. "You too?"

"Yes," Ryan responded, disregarding an ingrained instinct to maintain anonymity.

"What's he look like? I'll keep my eyes peeled."

"About six feet, 180 or so, brownish hair, fairly good looking, good shape, wearing khaki cargo shorts and a yellow T-shirt with a big black Y on the front."

"What does the Y stand for?"

Ryan chuckled. "Yale. He's kind of different from the mainstream. His name is Del Dickerson. Call me if you see him," he said, handing her his business card.

"I'm intrigued," Bunny gushed. "Let me hop over and fetch your Heineken."

Ryan scanned the room for his absent colleague, and scratched his ear. Where the hell are you, Del? And what are you doing?

## Chapter Three

"Looks clear," Chamberlin whispered to his cousin as he peered through a narrow door opening into the dark alley behind Captain Bill's Sea Shack. "Let's get him into the van quick."

"Big dude, Rufus. What ya think he weighs?"

"I'd guess about 175. Six feet at least."

"He fills up the bag, Beau. Did ya search him? Might have some cash on him. He won't need it where he's going."

"Good idea, Rufus. Just what I was thinking."

"Hmm," Beauregarde T. Chamberlin muttered a minute later. "No wallet, but sixty bucks in cash. I can sure use it."

"What do ya mean? We split it, thirty each."

"But I found it."

"And I told ya to search him."

"Okay, but I keep his watch."

"I don't know about you, Beau, you're greedy."

"Ain't greed good? That's what that guy said in my favorite movie."

"Whatever," Reynolds was saying as he watched Chamberlin jerk back suddenly, eyes bulging. "Sheeit! He's got a badge! We done got us a cop!"

"Lemme see," Reynolds demanded, seizing the shiny object and reading the engraved words: Federal Bureau of Investigation. "Keyriste! Ya done kilt a FBI agent!"

"ME! Yur just as capable."

"Culpable, Beau. Ya gotta use the right words."

"Shit! Who cares what ya call it? We got trouble!"

"Calm down. We gotta use our heads. We just do what we planned, and everything will be okay. We gotta dump the guy and hurry back to deliver the stuff to Ramon."

"Don't know why he wants it in two shipments," Chamberlin said, looking at the cardboard seafood boxes packed with plastic baggies of cocaine.

Reynolds stared at his cousin patronizingly. "In case one load gets seized, the other gets through—half a fortune."

Chamberlin shook his head. "The money's good, but what if I'm the one who's caught?"

"That's the risk of living the American dream, Beau. Ya wanta be rich, don't ya?"

"Well, yeah, but now we got a body to get rid of. I heard they give the death penalty for killing one of their guys," Chamberlin moaned. "I think I just pissed in my pants."

"Wondered what the smell was. Ya gotta learn to control yourself, Beau. Now give me a hand lifting the bag."

"What do I do with the badge? It's got a number on the back."

"Toss it in the fish trash. No one will find it there."

"Death penalty," Chamberlin mumbled repeatedly as they drove to the remote dock that berthed their 27-foot deep-sea fishing boat, *Lucky Lady*.

"No one around," Reynolds comforted as they hoisted the heavy body bag on to the stern of the boat. Within minutes, the twin 350 Mercury-powered engines had the *Lucky Lady* moving quietly seaward. "Good cloud cover," Reynolds called from his pilot seat. "Wur in good shape."

"Death penalty," Chamberlin murmured, eyeing the lumpy bag that appeared to be pulsating with periodic movement.

After forty minutes of bouncing through moderate waves, Reynolds cut back the engines and brought his vessel to a stop. "Looks like a good burial spot, Beau. No one in sight. Let's get him out of the bag."

"Why don't we leave him in the bag?"

"Beau, that's why the family don't think yur too bright. We leave him in the bag, anyone who finds him knows its foul play. Outside the bag, it looks like he hit his head and fell overboard from a fishing boat or something—an unfortunate accident. That is, if he's found. There's supposed to be a storm front coming through tonight. He could be far away with the sharks enjoying dinner in a few hours."

"Should we weight him down, Rufus? Help him sink fast?"

"No, no, Beau, ya still don't get it. It has to look like a accident."

"Oh," Chamberlin said, scratching his head and repeating the words death penalty as he helped Reynolds drag Special Agent Del Dickerson from the fish sack.

"Hey, a key ring fell outta the bag, Rufus. What do we do with it?"

"Yur a great searcher, Beau," was the sarcastic reply. "We gotta be more thorough if we wanta avoid the gas chamber. Toss it overboard."

"Gas chamber" Chamberlin moaned, throwing the keys into the sea.

"Good luck," Reynolds said, as he and Chamberlin

shoved the unconscious man overboard.

* * *

Chilled Atlantic Ocean water had only minimal impact on Del's body temperature, but not on his legendary luck. As he floated away from the *Lucky Lady*, a large rusted spike protruding from a piece of floating driftwood snagged the sleeve of his soggy T-shirt, maintaining his buoyancy. His still unconscious body floated south with the tide.

## Chapter Four

CAROLINA BEACH

Lucas Davis was making his early-morning collection from the restaurants and bars that provided a modest living in his resort community. Never know what you might find in the trash, he was reminding himself as he emptied the overflowing receptacle from Captain Bill's Sea Shack. Always check before dumping, he remembered, scanning the mound of seashells and other food remains. Two rings and a gold wristwatch adorning his hands bore testimony to his diligence. His eyes suddenly focused on a shiny object projecting from a fish head. Gloved fingers quickly extracted the object that he studied with excitement. "A badge," he muttered, reading the wording. "Holy smokes!" he uttered audibly, "an FBI Agent's badge! Bet the guy's looking like hell for it."

Good citizen Davis retrieved his cell phone from the pocket of his splattered work apron and called his local law enforcement officer. "Just found something interesting," he told Deputy Sheriff Lyle Lawson. "An FBI Agent's badge. Got a number on the back."

Within minutes, the graying officer rolled up in his black Ford and was examining the badge. "Good find, Lucas. I'll assume custody, and contact Brad Evans, the FBI agent who covers this territory. He'll know what to do with it. Came from behind Captain Bill's, eh? Not a good place to lose anything," he added, with a shake of his head. "Brad might like to ask some questions there."

## BALD HEAD ISLAND, NORTH CAROLINA

"It's so peaceful and serene," Leigh Daly remarked to her close friend as the middle-aged women walked on the sandy beach of the unique tiny island projecting defiantly into the Atlantic Ocean. Sandpipers scurried on tiny legs in the gentle waves lapping at the nearby shore. Random seagulls swooped gracefully overhead, highlighted against a dramatic blue sky.

"A wonderful retreat from the world's woes," Jenny Malone replied wistfully as she sidestepped a pink-tinted seashell recently deposited by the undulating surf.

*Captain Charlie's Porch* - by Sarah Hasty Williams

"How fortunate we are to be surrounded by such beauties of nature—the Blue Heron and White Ibis, to say nothing of the adorable turtles. Truly God's blessings to enjoy and appreciate. Quite a change from that storm last night."

"Kept me awake," Daly said, "but I felt safe in your cousin's cottage. It's so generous of her to let us spend some time at her beautiful place—some cottage."

Malone laughed. "*Cottage* doesn't quite fit a three story house with five bedrooms, but, she said we needed a comfortable place to rest and recover."

"You're doing great," Daly assured, referencing the recent accidental death of Malone's Naval officer husband that suddenly left her a grieving widow at a premature age.

"Thanks to your support, Leigh. You went through it much too early in life, and have adjusted admirably. What a shock you had, losing your FBI agent husband at such a young age."

"Hey, that's life," Daly said with a shrug. "No one said it would be a bowl of cherries."

"You make lemonade out of lemons," Malone praised. "Thanks for helping me cope."

"Isn't that what friends are for?"

"And you're the best, and I like your bromides."

"Old but true sayings, Jenny. Like fine wine. Speaking of that, when does Happy Hour start?"

Malone laughed. "A little early for that, but it has to be cocktail time somewhere. Maybe we should hurry back to the cottage."

The light-hearted banter continued as the pair strolled along the pristine beach. "So here we are," Daly reflected, "a couple of middle-aged gals, remembering the good times, and wondering what the future will bring."

"Well, we know that life can be full of surprises," Malone responded, looking ahead at the deserted beach. "What's that?" she wondered.

Daly adjusted her sunglasses. "It's big—a shark or something?"

Hurrying forward, the women were soon abreast of a water-logged body being nudged ashore by gentle wave action.

"It's a man!" Daly shouted.
"Is he dead?" Malone questioned.

\* \* \*

## WASHINGTON, D.C.

Anna Chen, Del Dickerson's Amerasian fiancée, sounded worried when her cell call to Kevin Ryan was answered. "I haven't been able to reach him, Kevin."

"Me neither," Ryan replied. "We were supposed to meet for dinner last evening, but he never showed up. I've been asking around with no luck. There's several places in town to stay, but he didn't register at any of them as far as I can learn. We met very early yesterday morning to go fishing, so he could have stopped some place along the trip from D.C. Hell, he could have slept in his car—you know how unpredictable he can be."

"Yes, you never know what he might do. He promised to call me last night. As you know, I'm here to testify in the fraud trial of former Congressman Walters who we nabbed in the SPYTRAP investigation. I have to be here another day, but I'll hurry down there as soon as I can. I'm so worried, Kevin."

"He's a survivor, Anna. Don't forget the grand finale of SPYTRAP, when he dropped from a helicopter onto a sinking raft on the Potomac River."

"I know, Kevin. You were there. Del and I have been through other life-threatening situations, and it's truly amazing we're both still alive. He's enjoyed fabulous good luck. But doesn't the cat have so many lives?"

"Let's pray he has several left, Anna. I'll let you

know anything I learn."

Ryan glanced out his motel window, eyes fixed on a black cat prancing regally across the parking lot. How many lives do you guys have? was his somber thought.

## Chapter Five

<u>COLOMBIA, SOUTH AMERICA</u>

"Isn't she a wonder, Captain?" the burly Russian engineer asked.

"Indeed, Serge. Your countrymen have lived up to their promises."

"And it will earn you a fortune when you deliver its cargo to the decadent Americans begging to feed their habits."

The two men stood on the steamy shore of a narrow river snaking through the thick jungle, admiring the sleek blue hull of a 60-foot long submarine. "Two million dollars of high-tech design and electronics, Captain. Ready for your long journey?"

"Si, Colonel," Carlos Alvarez replied. "I'm told it will earn at least four hundred million dollars on American streets."

"Their hunger is insatiable, Captain, so why shouldn't we help the pompous capitalists speed their destruction?" His snicker was pronounced. "Are you prepared to sail?"

"My crew and I await arrival of the cargo."

"You will have your supply tomorrow, Captain, so start counting your money—you will be a rich man with half your payment before you leave, and another fifty thousand Yankee dollars upon delivery of your cargo."

The dark brown eyes of Captain Carlos Alvarez glowed with anticipation.

"Of course," the Russian added, "your other crewmen will only earn a pittance."

"A few hundred dollars when they have nothing is a fortune to them," Alvarez said in his heavy accent, "and rank does have its privilege, you know. I'm the one who knows how to operate the controls and instruments, thanks to my training by the Colombian Navy, the bastards who destroyed my career with their putrid charges. I could have been an Admiral if they hadn't plotted against me. I was working up to command the Colombian National Navy *ARC GLORIA*, the beautiful three-masted tall ship that trains midshipmen, when someone betrayed me. One of the women aboard claimed I raped her. Hell, they were giving it away, hard to avoid with the constant music and a few shots of tequila. Everyone was doing her. Anyway, she got knocked up and they blamed me-- said they had to make an example and booted me out."

"You're in a much more lucrative profession now," the husky Russian assured, adding, "the workers you hired to assemble the parts my engineers brought to this remote place did a good job. They earned their wages. After you pay them the money I gave you, provide them with a good dinner, and mucho tequila."

Alavarez, nodded agreement.

"Then," the Russian said through grim lips, "kill them."

The Colombian's eyes sparkled with understanding as he again nodded agreement. "It will be done," he affirmed, mentally totaling the payments he would eventually retrieve from the dead men.

"Bon voyage," the Russian concluded, moving his thick body towards a waiting powerboat, its muffled

Yamaha engine purring in readiness. Truly a jungle, he muttered as he waved farewell.

## CAROLINA BEACH

New Hanover County Deputy Sheriff Lyle Lawson felt energized as he concluded his call to FBI Special Agent Brad Evans in the Wilmington, North Carolina, Resident Agency. Evans told him it should take mere minutes for headquarters in Washington to advise what agent had been issued badge number 6537, cautioning that it could be that of a former agent, or a long-lost item. A prompt return call was promised.

Lawson's wait was interrupted by another call, this one from a man who identified himself as FBI Special Agent Kevin Ryan, in town for a fishing expedition with a colleague who was now missing.

"Son," the crusty old Deputy said, "this must be FBI Day in Carolina Beach. I've got you folks coming and going," he said, proceeding to recount his conversation with the Wilmington agent. "Stay where you are. I'm coming right over. We need to put our heads together to solve this Federal case."

Haven't had this much action in weeks, Lawson thought, hurrying to his cruiser and rushing towards the Hampton Inn five blocks away.

Midway to the motel, Lawson got a message with the information from Wilmington: the badge number reported was issued to an active-duty agent named Delbert G. Dickerson. The dispatcher added that Special Agent Evans was en route from Wilmington.

Five minutes later, Lawson and Kevin Ryan were

shaking hands at the entrance of Room 105 of the Hampton Inn. "I've got a clue on your missing friend," Lawson said, producing badge number 6537. "I'm told it was issued to a Delbert Dickerson."

With escalating concern, Ryan studied the badge, interrupted by a cell call from Brad Evans, reporting he was about fifteen minutes away. Concluding the conversation with Evans, Ryan said, "An early official visit to Captain Bill's Sea Shack is in order."

"Can I join you?" Deputy Sheriff Lawson asked. "I've had that place on my radar for some time."

"Absolutely, sheriff. We couldn't do it without your cooperation. This is a team effort."

"While awaiting Brad's arrival, let's review what we know," Lawson suggested.

"Good idea," Ryan agreed. "I told you earlier that Del and I arranged to meet at the charter boat dock early in the morning. He walked up with a pouch containing his gun, cell phone, wallet, and creds, and asked me to lock it in the reinforced chest he knew I had in my trunk. He joked that he didn't want to be weighted down with all that stuff if we had to swim back."

"Did you see his car?" Lawson inquired.

"No, I didn't, come to think of it, but I last saw him driving a light blue Chrysler convertible. Anyway, my car was parked near the charter boat. I locked his stuff in my trunk and we hurried to board the boat. When we returned to the marina that afternoon, we walked a block or so to the nearest bar to quench our thirsts. I still had his stuff in my trunk, planning to return it when we met for dinner."

"Let's see if we can find his car," Lawson said, clicking on his phone and instructing his dispatcher to issue a lookout for a blue Chrysler convertible with Virginia plates. "Any chance he just could have driven home?" Lawson asked Ryan with a grin.

Ryan returned the smile. "He's unpredictable, Lyle, but not that far out. His badge was found here, you know."

"Just kidding, Kevin. Trying to lighten the atmosphere. I know it's a serious matter."

## Chapter Six

BALD HEAD ISLAND

"He's shaking and groaning, and he's got a big lump on the side of his head," Malone said, studying the body sprawled at their feet. "What should we do?"

"Call someone, I guess," Daly replied, "But who? There's hardly anyone around. It's off season. Do they even have ambulances on the island? All I've seen are electric carts."

"Must be a sheriff or something. My cousin would know what to do, but she won't be down from Northern Virginia for a few days. Maybe we should call 911, Leigh, but I didn't bring my cell phone."

"Me neither. We agreed to get away from those modern touches, but we have to do something—get him to shelter, but he's too heavy for us to carry," Malone said.

Daly's face brightened. "Your cousin's trailer—you know, the cart she tows behind her golf cart for supplies and such. We bring both from the cottage on the asphalt path. Unhitch it and roll it down to the beach. It looks light enough to roll easily over the sand. We load the guy onto it and haul him to the cottage."

"Brilliant, Leigh. I'll get it. You stay with the guy. He sure is shaking."

"Yeah, we need to warm him up," Daly said, removing her blue felt jacket and draping it over the shivering body. "Bring some blankets, and hurry."

\* \* \*

Fifteen minutes later, Malone returned with the cart, unhitched the trailer and rolled it to the beach. After an energetic struggle with the sodden body, the women managed to heft the form onto the trailer, legs dangling out the back. With wool blankets tucked around their mystery guest, the women rushed their rescue vehicle towards the cottage and reached the cottage's wooden walkway where they studied the entrance stairs. "Almost there!" Daly exclaimed. "Let's get him into the first floor den, then we need a drink."

With fading bursts of energy, the exhausted pair managed to hoist their unexpected guest up the stairs into the cottage and onto a daybed.

"Whew! We did it!" Daly rejoiced.

"Is he still breathing?" Malone asked.

"Barely, it seems."

"We should get him out of his wet clothes, Leigh."

"Yeah, not much of those—shorts, T-shirt and tennis shoes."

"Maybe we should check for other wounds. You were a nurse, Leigh, why don't you do the honors?"

"After we check his vitals, Jenny. Does your cousin have first aid equipment?"

"My cousin has one of everything," Malone assured, hurrying away, to return a minute later with a medical kit with blood pressure monitor. "Go at it, nursie."

"126 over 78," Daly announced minutes later, "pulse 62. Pretty good for what he must have gone through. The guy's blessed with a strong constitution."

"So far so good, Leigh. Now for the search."

Daly nodded agreement and proceeded to remove a pair of New Balance running shoes. "Size twelve," she announced, dropping them to the floor. "Now the T-shirt," she said, tugging at the yellow fabric. "Wonder what the big black Y stands for?"

"Yellowstone, Youngstown, Yugoslavia? Could be anything. He might have fallen off a ship, Leigh. Could be Yale, my brother had one that looked like that."

"Boola, boola" Daly said, removing the garment. "Extra-large. Maybe we should sing Yale's *The Whiffenpoof Song*. Might wake him up."

"Or finish him off with our voices, Leigh. Keep going on the shorts, and check his pockets."

"Nothing there," Daly reported a minute later, studying the Jockey shorts that remained in place. Suppose we should?"

Malone nodded. "Could have additional wounds. I doubt if he would mind us exploring, since he appears almost dead."

"Guess you're right," Daly said, pulling the soggy undergarment off. "Size 36," she declared.

"Hmm, quite well endowed," Malone observed with a flush of facial reddening.

"Yeah," Daly agreed, hastening to cover their patient with warm blankets. "Notice anything else?"

"Like what?"

"The light band of skin circling his left wrist, where I'm guessing a watch previously reposed. I suspect that our guest may have been relieved of it before he went swimming. Along with the knot on his head, it may not have been an accident that he ended up in the ocean."

Malone's eyes widened. "That's a clever deduction. You're a born detective."

"Maybe I'm overly suspicious, Jenny, but you don't live with an FBI Agent for fifteen years without absorbing some of his skills. Now, I believe it's time to open that bottle of wine and call 911."

## CAROLINA BEACH

Special Agent Brad Evans from the FBI's Wilmington Resident Agency arrived, and after mutual introductions, the trio of law enforcement officers proceeded to Captain Bill's Sea Shack.

"Well, hello, Lyle. Glad to see you. Haven't had the pleasure for a while. Who are your friends?" Captain Bill Andrews asked, greeting the Deputy Sheriff from his chair at a back table. His narrow smile radiated questionable sincerity.

"Hi, Bill," Lawson responded.

Evans and Ryan introduced themselves, displaying their credentials.

"My, <u>two</u> FBI agents. This must be serious," Captain Bill said with mock concern.

"We're looking for my missing colleague," Ryan said. "He was last seen here with me yesterday afternoon. I called back, and a woman said she didn't remember seeing us."

"That would have been Wanda. She was on duty all day, and she's here now. Wanda!" he shouted at a red-haired woman lounging on a barstool. "Come here!"

Snuffing out a cigarette, the thirty-some year-old waitress headed their way. Long bare legs rose to brief denim shorts, topped with a snug, low-cut white T-shirt displaying the slogan *GRAB A COLD ONE AT*

*CAPTAIN BILL'S.* Her ample braless breasts swayed provocatively below the thin fabric that minimally concealed prominent nipples.

"These gents are looking for a missing friend they say visited us yesterday," Captain Bill said. "They wonder if you remember him."

Ryan provided Del's description. "You served us," he added.

Wanda exchanged looks with Captain Bill, then turned back to Ryan. "We was really busy," she said, with a hint of nervousness. "Sorry, my memory isn't too good."

"Don't you remember me?" Ryan persisted.

Wanda glanced again at Captain Bill, and licked her upper lip. "Sorry, mister."

"Well," Captain Bill spoke up, "guess you have the wrong establishment, and Wanda needs to get back to work."

"Thanks for your cooperation," Ryan said in a tone of disbelief, handing the woman his business card. "Call me if your memory returns."

Captain Bill studied his wristwatch. "I have another appointment, so if you have no more questions..."

"Thank you for your time," Special Agent Evans said.

"Always happy to assist law enforcement," Captain Bill stated with a barely concealable smirk.

"I expect to see you again," Ryan said in a promising tone.

Captain Bill smiled. "Always glad for the business."

"And you can be sure I'll be seeing you," Deputy Sheriff Lawson added.

\*　\*　\*

"Lying bastards!" Ryan exclaimed with disgust to his companions as they conferred back at the Hampton Inn.

"I'll be keeping a sharp eye on his joint," Lawson assured, clearing his throat. "If y'all pardon my country boy language, Captain Bill is a first-class asshole. He's a piss-poor fishing boat captain, and a disgrace to the U.S. Navy—calls himself a Captain! I've know the scumbag for years. Best he did in the Navy until they booted him out with a dishonorable discharge was Captain of the head. He's a real loser, but makes a living with some highly questionable activities. We've had years of problems at his shack—fights, drugs, hustling, you name it. The dregs of the area hang out there. Wanda has probably shared her favors with every guy in town, plus an army of visitors."

"She rather effectively advertised her offerings," Evans noted wryly.

"I don't judge her, fellows," Lawson remarked. "Girl has to make a living, and she's scared of Bill, but don't expect anything but bullshit from that place."

"Our files include a few tips about drug deals at Captain Bill's," Evans interjected. "We'll afford it increased attention."

Ryan shook his head. "Damn! We're no closer to finding Del," he was deploring when his cell phone rang. The message was brief: "Need to talk to you about your missing friend," a husky female-sounding voice whispered. "I'll call back."

Ryan related the message to his associates. "Sounded like Wanda."

## Chapter Seven

<u>BALD HEAD ISLAND</u>

"I know it's early, but I think we've earned it," Leigh Daly said, uncorking a bottle of Kendall-Jackson chardonnay.

"Didn't we agree it has to be happy hour somewhere?" Jenny Malone said, extracting two large glasses from a cabinet. "Pour."

"Maybe we should offer a glass to the guy," Daly said. "Might revive him. Wonder what his name is?"

"How about calling him Y in the meantime," Malone suggested.

"Good idea, Jenny, and we better check on him."

"Shouldn't we call 911, Leigh?"

"Let's see how he's doing. Maybe he'll come to, and we'll at least know who he is."

"Whatever you say," Malone agreed, leading the way into the adjoining den.

"He's mumbling something," Malone exclaimed, hurrying to the man's side.

"What's he saying?" Daly asked, leaning close.

"Sounded like Ann, or and ... could be sand."

"And he's starting to squirm around, Jenny. Oh my! Are you seeing what I'm seeing?"

With widening eyes, the women saw the blanket covering the man's abdomen steadily rise until it projected like a circus tent pole under the big top. "Well, it sure looks like he's alive," Daly managed to say.

"He's moving his head, too," Malone observed, "and his eyes are blinking."

"Hey, mister, good to see you waking up," were Daly's welcoming words.

The man's fluttering eyes remained open as they focused on the two women and he surveyed his surroundings. "Who are you?" he asked, "and where am I?"

"Leigh Daly and Jenny Malone, and you're on Bald Head Island. Who are you?"

The man's cloudy eyes closed momentarily, and he licked his lips. "I'm thirsty."

"Of course," Malone said, "and we'll get you some water right away, but what's your name?"

"I'm, I'm..." the man mumbled. "Oh, my head hurts," he said, reaching to touch the large lump on the left side of his head.

"Do you know how that happened?" Daly pursued, "and tell us your name?"

"My name is ..." the man said, staring at the women with obvious concern. "I can't remember. And, where is Bald Head Island? And where are my clothes?" he added, moving his hands beneath the blankets.

Daly looked at Malone. "Amnesia. I've seen it before in trauma cases. Hopefully, it's temporary."

"I'll get your water, and how about some warm soup?" Malone asked.

The man nodded. "Yes. Hungry. What day is it?"

"Thursday," Malone replied, "eleven-thirty a.m."

The man glanced reflexively at his left wrist.

"Your watch is missing. Do you remember losing it?" Daly asked.

The man's head shook.

"Do we call 911 now?" Malone asked.

"And tell them we have a man with no name? Now that he's awake, let's see if we can learn more about him before we call. Maybe we can jolt his recollection."

"Oh, I've got a hell of a headache," the man groaned, as he sat up in his bed, causing his blanket to drop to his waist.

"Look at those muscles," Malone muttered to Daly as she passed to secure water. "Maybe we should keep him here for a while."

"Oh you devil," Daly jested in reply. "Well perhaps a day or so?" she added.

## SOUTHPORT, NORTH CAROLINA

Beau Chamberlin and Rufus Reynolds sat at a remote table in Sam's Bar, nursing mugs of draft Budweiser while recounting their recent deliveries to Ramon's Fresh Catch, a seafood store located a block away.

"Still don't know why we don't deliver it all at once," Beau groused. "Save gas."

"I told ya before why," Rufus replied. "Insurance, in case the cops intercept one of our loads."

Chamberlin took another swallow of beer and grabbed a honey-glazed chicken wing from the basket before them. "Haven't seen any suspicious people hanging around, except that guy we dropped in the drink. Wonder where he ended up?"

"Shark bait, probably," Reynolds scoffed. "What happens to nosey people. We need to concentrate on our business here. You know Ramon expects us to deliver without problems. We better not mention the guy that went swimming."

"Okay, Rufus, don't want to rile him up. Spics got hot tempers, but he's sure got a smooth operation—regular seafood in the front of his store, our stuff in the back. Takes brains."

"There's bigger brains, Beau—the guy he reports to. We're not supposed to know anything about him."

"I heard he lives on Old Baldy, Rufus."

Reynolds glared at his cousin. "Better forget that bit of gossip, Beau. Could be bad for your health."

"I'm in great health," Chamberlin declared, pounding his chest. Reynolds shook his head. The head, dummy, the head, was his thought as he picked up his beer mug.

BALD HEAD ISLAND

"Fresh catch arrived," was the cryptic message telephoned by Ramon Montez to former U.S. Navy Commander Randolph, (commonly known as Randy) King, in the office-den of King's secluded residence on the tiny island.

Ramon is a trusted aide, King mused, recalling a host of junior officers who had served him during a once-promising military career, abruptly aborted upon a court martial conviction for multiple illegal acts. "Bastards," he mumbled, reflecting on recurring visions of himself wearing an Admiral's stars. Thoughts flashed back to his years at Annapolis, where he graduated in the upper third of his class, then a variety of postings until his involvement with an international arms dealer offering intriguing financial inducements for favorable contract approvals. The two years of confinement at Leavenworth penitentiary passed quickly, he recalled, without the constant carping of his socially ambitious wife, a Baltimore debutante who he met at an Academy dance. She had filed for divorce the day he was charged. Good riddance, was his lingering thought, as he remembered their bitter, alcohol-fueled arguments over money and mutual infidelities. Now, his reminisces continued, my new business returns unbelievable profits, without daily harangues from that bitch. King sat back in his navy blue and gold recliner and smiled with satisfaction. All this made possible by one of my old navy buddies with Russian connections. Go Navy!

WASHINGTON, D.C.

Anna Chen sounded distraught on her evening call to Kevin Ryan. "No word at all, Kevin?"

"Brad Evans, the R.A. from Wilmington and I have talked to almost everyone in town—no one claims to have seen him, but we're convinced the staff at Captain Bill's Sea Shack are stonewalling us. That's where I last saw Del. We're digging into activities at Captain Bill's, a low-life dive. We still need to talk with a couple of fisherman of poor repute who hang out there. How's the trial going?"

Ryan's question served to momentarily divert Anna's attention from concerns about her fiancé as she reported the status of the case that critically involved her in the FBI's SPYTRAP investigation. "One more witness to testify," she informed, "and then I hope to be excused so I can join the search for Del. I am so worried, Kevin."

"Let's think positive, Anna. You above all know how he invariably lands on his feet. He's probably luxuriating in a fancy abode with no phone. Imagine the possibilities."

"Thanks for the encouragement, Kevin. You haven't lost your gift of Irish blarney."

"We'll find him, Anna. Keep the faith," Ryan said

"We need a break," Ryan was saying to Evans when his cell phone rang again.

"Can't talk long," a familiar female voice whispered against a background of barroom-sounding noise, "but you should check on two guys who frequently use Captain Bill's back room—Beau and Rufus." A distinct click followed.

Ryan turned to Evans. "Wanda, I'm sure. She gave us two names before the call ended abruptly." A worried frown engulfed his face. "I'm going back to Captain Bill's," he said with grim conviction. "Hate to be lied to."

"Roger that," Evans replied. "I was briefed on your background, and look forward to observing a former SEAL in action. Let's go."

# Chapter Eight

CAROLINA BEACH

"Hello, Mr. Andrews," Special Agent Kevin Ryan greeted as he and fellow agent Brad Evans entered Captain Bill's Sea Shack.

"I'm usually known as Captain Bill," Andrews proclaimed. "You must have been snooping in private records."

"Public records," Evans corrected. "It's called due diligence. We know who you are, and your record."

Andrews snickered. "You're by yourselves. Don't you need my good friend, the sheriff, protecting you?"

"He's doing other work on your activities," Evans said. "I believe we can protect ourselves. We'd like to talk to two of your patrons, Beau and Rufus."

"Who? I kind of remember a pair of customers by those names."

"You seem to have a convenient memory, Andrews," Ryan said. "Your waitress, Wanda, also seems to suffer from that affliction. We want to talk to her again."

"She doesn't work here anymore," Captain Bill responded coolly. "So, what else can I help you with?" Andrews asked, a nervous twitch flickering below his left eye.

"Start by telling the truth," Ryan said, rising to his feet. "We're looking for a missing Federal agent, and we won't stop searching until we find him. Is that clear enough?"

"Is that a threat?" Andrew blustered.

"Consider it a promise," Ryan said grimly as he picked up a wooden chair and smashed it over an adjacent table. "Whoops," he declared as the fragments fell to the floor. "Some of your furnishings seem to be a bit fragile. Get the message?" Andrews sat stunned, tugging blank-faced at his collar, staring at the splintered chair.

"Tell Beau and Rufus we'll be back," Evans said as they left the restaurant.

"What the hell was that?" a grizzled bar patron asked his drinking buddy as they watched the agents depart.

"Just another day at Captain Bill's," his partner replied, signaling for a refill.

\* \* \*

"Who said former SEALS got soft?" Evans asked Ryan with a grin as they climbed into the Bureau car.

## KURE BEACH, NORTH CAROLINA

"Who made the call?" Deputy Sheriff Lyle Lawson asked his assistant, Brian Stewart, who stared numbly at the body crumpled next to a green dumpster.

"A tourist who was parked at the rear of the restaurant. Leaving after a late dinner. He's sitting in the back seat of my cruiser. Pretty shook up. Said he didn't notice anything unusual until he turned on his headlights and saw the body."

"Any ID?" Lawson asked, moving forward to examine the crime scene. "Oh shit," he cursed as his flashlight beam illuminated the victim. "We both know who it is."

"Yeah," Stewart concurred, "and look at what was used to strangle her."

Lawson peered closer at the garment wrapped around the woman's neck. Fragments of words-- rab, Col, and Bil, were partially visible. Lawson's memory flashed to the T-shirt he recently saw with its provocative slogan, *Grab A Cold One At Captain Bills*. God have mercy on Wanda's soul, Lawson murmured. "Looks like our problems are escalating," he said to Stewart. "You call the medical examiner. I'll notify the FBI agents."

## BALD HEAD ISLAND

"We're calling you **Y** until we learn who you are," Daly said to their guest who was eagerly slurping from a bowl of chicken noodle soup. "Do you know what the Y stands for?"

Del shook his head and studied the T-shirt he had pulled back on, along with his other garments that felt cozily warm after a quick dryer spin. A confused look lingered on his face.

"Could it be YALE?" Malone probed.

Another shake of his head followed. "Don't know," he said.

"Do you have any idea how you ended up in the water?" Daly asked. "You mumbled Ann, or and, or sand, when we found you. Do those words stir any thoughts?"

Del paused, searching for words. "Sorry, but

thanks for the soup. Do you have any more?"

"Right away," Malone said, picking up the empty bowl. "Would you also like some chocolate pudding?"

"That would be wonderful, and might you have something for my headache, like aspirin or Tylenol?"

"But, of course," Daly apologized, "we should have given you that right away."

"You're both very kind," Del said with an appreciative smile. "Where did you say we are?"

"Bald Head Island, North Carolina. It's near Wilmington."

"Isn't that in Delaware?" Del asked.

"There's one there too," Daly said. "Is that where you're from, or did you live there? This might be a breakthrough."

Del shook his head, and thanked Malone for the Tylenol tablet. "I don't know," he finally said.

"We don't want to exhaust you with all our questions," Daly said, "but we want to find out who you are so you can be reunited with your loved ones."

Del nodded. "Me too. I understand, and thank you. Ask away."

"Do you remember what you do for a living?"

Del looked at his hands. "No calluses. Doesn't look like I'm a laborer."

"You have an athletic build, and big muscles," Malone said. "A professional athlete perhaps?"

Del shrugged. "Tylenol's helping, thanks."

"Do you have a wife or girlfriend?" Daly questioned with a smile. "There's no wedding ring on your finger, and no mark indicating that one might have been there."

41

"Gee, I don't know."

"How old are you?" Daly asked. "You look about thirty-five. Do you remember your date of birth?"

Del just stared helplessly as Daly continued. "Are you a fisherman?"

"Fish ...?" Del said, seeming to search for understanding before shaking his head.

"You sound like you might have an Eastern accent," Daly observed, "does Massachusetts, New York, New Jersey, Connecticut, Vermont, New Hampshire, Maine mean anything?"

Del pondered the question. "Connecticut sounds kind of familiar."

Daly clapped her hands. " Bravo. Maybe we're breaking through. Anything more about Connecticut?"

Del shook his head. "I'm sorry. I wish I could be of more help," he said as his eyes began to close. "Tired," he said.

Daly looked at Malone. "We need to let him rest. He's been through a lot."

"Yeah," Malone said with a grin. "You wore him out with your interrogation, Detective Colombo. Should we call 911 now?"

"Let's leave him rest for a bit, then take one more shot before we make the call. There has to be a breakthrough point. Meanwhile, is there any wine left?"

Malone poured the remains into their glasses. "To Y," she toasted. "Quite a healthy catch."

Daly sipped from her glass. "Has he fallen asleep?"

Malone rose to peer into the adjacent room, returning with raised eyebrows. "Come see, I do believe he's gaining strength."

"You're definitely right," Daly said, studying the blanket steadily rising over Y's lower body. "Sort of reminds one of the nearby Cape Fear lighthouse."

Malone gulped. "Tallest thing around, they say. I do believe we need to open another bottle of wine in tribute."

## Chapter Nine

CAROLINA BEACH

It was a somber group of law enforcement officers conferring in Ryan's room at the Hampton Inn. Deputy Sheriff Lawson had just concluded his report on the status of the murder investigation of Wanda Somerset. "She had only been dead a couple of hours when she was found. Death by asphyxiation, the coroner ruled. Crushed windpipe, powerful hands, were some of his findings," Lawson related.

"Your quiet little community has suddenly become not so peaceful," Ryan said to the sheriff in a sympathetic tone. "I'm sure you don't experience a missing FBI agent and a murder very often."

"That's for sure," Lawson agreed, "and I'm grateful for your help."

"It's a team effort," Ryan declared.

"The forensics team from our Wilmington office is currently helping process the crime scene," Evans added. "Powerful hands, the M.E. said. Fit anyone in particular? Perhaps a commercial fisherman?"

Lawson nodded towards the agents. "Yeah, I calculate a talk with Beau Chamberlin and Rufus Reynolds is long overdue. I'm putting out an APB right away."

Completing his instructions to his dispatcher, Lawson's eyebrows rose as he listened, interjecting several questions. He raised his thumb in the direction of the agents and concluded the call. "Some good news," he said, "canvassing officers located your agent's car."

"Where?" Ryan asked.

"About two blocks from the charter dock, parked on a side street. Locked. I ordered it towed to our secure lot. What say we go check it out? Guess he didn't drive off after all," he added with a smile.

"Told you, sheriff," Ryan laughed. "Let's go."

## BALD HEAD ISLAND

"While we're waiting for Y to wake up, what are we having for dinner?" Daly asked.

"Well, it won't be seafood, Leigh, since our planned ferry boat trip to Southport to load up got sunk when the mystery man washed up at our feet. Ramon's has the freshest catch around."

"My mouth was watering for it, Jenny. It's always so good."

"It's worth the trip over, and I'm amazed at the prices—beats anything available on the island. I can see why the store is always so busy. The word must have gotten around. You always see cars with out-of-state licenses parked out front. It'll be worth the wait, but for tonight it's something frozen from the fridge. I imagine Y will be happy with anything. He appears to have quite an appetite. Wonder how he's doing?"

"Still asleep," Malone reported after a peek into the den. "He seems to be mumbling. Maybe having a dream."

*  *  *

Little more than a mile away, former navy Commander Randy King was gazing fondly at the sturdy waxed cardboard box marked SHRIMP, just delivered to him by Ramon Montez, proprietor of Ramon's Fresh Seafood. The wiry native of Colombia flashed his trademark bright smile as he relaxed with his employer on King's sheltered screened porch, watching a sinking sun descend towards the horizon. "No need to refrigerate the contents," Montez jested in his musical accent.

"No," King agreed, lifting the lid to view the array of U.S. currency cramming the box. "You deducted your share, of course."

"Yes, thank you, Commander. You are a generous benefactor."

"Your trip was smooth?" King asked.

"Yes, my Sea-Doo brought me swiftly and quietly from Southport to your dock near the Old Boat House. Twenty minutes at most. We just skimmed along. My little jewel doesn't draw much water."

"Splendid, Ramon. We have a mutually profitable operation, one that will remain so if there aren't any problems. We don't have any, do we?"

"I make sure of that, sir."

"Your couriers are reliable?" King pressed. "We can't permit a weak link—you know the reality that a chain is only as strong as its weakest link?"

"I feel we are absolutely strong all along the chain," Montez professed with confidence, suppressing a fleeting sense of uncertainty.

"Good," King said, replacing the cover. "I'll count it later. Now, how about a Kobe beef steak? I hate seafood."

Montez smiled. "You live well, Commander. How

do you maintain such a grand palace?"

"Like we said, my faithful lieutenant, eliminate the weak links. I rely on my own abilities and limit access to my secrets. The navy taught me to pick up after myself. I only allow a cleaning woman into my territory once a week. She's a simple soul, and I keep a keen eye on her. I don't let her into my communications room. No problem." Turning, and pointing to the West, King declared, "Look at that brilliant sunset! How could life be better?"

## CAROLINA BEACH

Ryan, Evans, and Lawson had retreated to what was popularly considered the best restaurant in town for what the sheriff called their attitude adjustment hour.

"Great idea," Ryan announced as they settled at the bar. Evans voiced agreement, saying "guess I can handle a soft drink before my thirty-minute drive home."

Ryan looked askance at his fellow agent. "We're not in fairyland, Brad. Three beers," he called to Bunny who was hurrying over to take their order.

"What's going on at your Washington headquarters?" Lawson queried Ryan.

Ryan rolled his eyes. "Some rotten apples rose to the top, but you can bet your ass the heart and soul employees won't permit destruction of a great organization."

"Good to hear," Lawson said. "We've depended on your leadership. You sent me to the National Academy, you know."

"Only the best of local officers are selected to attend, Lyle. You obviously measured up for what is often called the West Point of Law Enforcement."

Lawson tipped his mug to his companions. "The thin blue line is under attack, my friends. Without us we have a jungle."

"I heard that," Bunny interjected, "and I think you guys are great. Drinks on me."

"Thanks, Bunny," Ryan said, "but you work too hard. We're concerned about another barmaid."

"Wanda? Heard about that. Didn't know her well, but I know she was supporting a couple of kids, and didn't have much option but to work at Captain Bill's."

"The sheriff will find out who's responsible, and justice will be served," Ryan assured. Turning towards a side room of the main restaurant where a private party was assembling, he added, "Looks like you will have a busy evening."

"Yeah, some tourists just rolled in. They look like a fun bunch. They have a big dog with them," she said, before hurrying away to fill a large bar order, leaving the troubled trio to sip their drinks.

While the men glanced at the evening news being reported on an overhead TV, a loud bark sounded from the nearby party room, followed shortly by a blur of action as a man chased a large black Labrador bounding through a half-open doorway. The dog was headed directly for Ryan, who stared in disbelief from his barstool. "Rambo!" he shouted as the wiggling Lab affectionately licked his hand.

# Chapter Ten

CAROLINA BEACH

"What are you doing here?" Ryan asked with disbelief, addressing his former boss from Northern Virginia, Andy Dutton.

"Going on vacation," Dutton replied, pumping Ryan's hand. "How about you? This is the last place I would expect to find you."

"Likewise, boss, it's been months since we concluded the SPYTRAP special in Tysons Corner."

"A lot's happened since then, Kevin. You went on the Inspection Staff, and they named me one of the Special Agents in Charge at the Manassas R.A."

"Long overdue, Andy. But what brings you here?"

"Pure vacation, Kevin. Before I retire next month."

"Finally taking that Lockheed Martin offer, eh? About time. You'll triple your salary."

"It's not about the money, Kevin. The organization isn't what it was before the politicians polluted the water."

"I know what you mean, Andy."

"We're depending on people like you to restore the luster, Kevin."

"You can be sure we'll do our best, but tell me what brings you to Carolina Beach?"

"We're headed for Bald Head Island. Its only a few miles south of here and several people have told us that it's a hidden gem. We rented a cottage for a week for the whole family—our extended one. They'll be thrilled to see you. We're looking forward to a relaxed, no-pressure vacation. What about you?"

Ryan released a small smile. "Boss, you won't believe what we have cooking here. Sit down, and keep a firm grip on your scotch and water."

Before Ryan could mention their problems, Dutton's wife, Lydia, appeared in pursuit of Rambo. "What a delightful surprise," the comely matron exclaimed. "Never expected to see such a special friend in these parts. Come and greet the rest of our jolly group. All we need is Del. Have you heard from him lately?"

"Let's go and say hello," Ryan said, without answering her question," and meet my friends," he continued, proceeding to introduce Evans and the sheriff.

"Glad to see you," Dutton whispered to Ryan as they approached the party room. "I've felt a bit outnumbered for male presence, except for Rambo."

"Poor guy," Ryan joked, waving at two vivacious women who would handily win most beauty contests.

"Folks," Ryan said, entering the room, "I'm overwhelmed to see all of you again, and want to introduce my two outstanding colleagues, Deputy Sheriff Lyle Lawson, of New Hanover County, and Special Agent Brad Evans of the nearby Wilmington R.A. We're working together on some major problems which I'll detail in a minute, but first I'd like you to introduce yourselves to my friends."

The tall striking brunet was the first to speak. "I am Natalie Rostov, rescued from Russian enslavement by Del Dickerson. We were almost murdered together not long ago. I'd do anything for him. I consider him my bosom buddy," she concluded with a slight giggle.

A taller, curvaceous blonde followed, identifying

herself as Tanya Tamarof. "I, too, was given the opportunity of a new life in America thanks to Del. Natalie and I now operate a Tae Kwon Do studio in Northern Virginia. We crack the whip on our students," she said with a laugh. "Our friend, Olga, operates a snack bar in our establishment. We're living the American dream."

Dutton's sturdy housekeeper then jumped up. "I am Olga Servadova, and I make good goulash, but where is Del? He owes me a pot handle."

While the group laughed, Ryan whispered to Evans and Lawson, "Natalie and Tanya were Russian honey pots. Del facilitated their defection--quite a feat. Olga was a strategic bonus."

Regaining attention, Ryan addressed his audience in a serious tone. "Everyone asks about Del, and where he is. The answer is we don't know. He and I came down here on a fishing trip, and he disappeared after a day on the water. There's been an all-out search for him, and we suspect he may have been the victim of foul play. His badge was found in discarded trash near an establishment he was last seen patronizing. A waitress who served him there was recently found strangled to death. Sorry to relate such grim news."

The previous light-hearted atmosphere plunged. Even Rambo appeared downcast.

Dutton stood and eyed his companions. "Well, it looks like this will be a working vacation, folks. Let's get to work and find Del, and solve the murder. It's what we do, you know."

"Da" (yes), Nadia said.

Tanya added her support. "Konechao" (of course).

"Pozhallstah," (please) Olga confirmed.

"Arf," Rambo certified.

## WASHINGTON, D.C.

"The jury delivered a unanimous verdict of guilty against Jason," Anna Chen reported to Kevin Ryan on their evening call, after Ryan apologetically informed Del's fiancée that there was no progress in finding him. "But," Ryan continued, "local police found Del's car, parked near the charter boat dock. We processed it thoroughly, but didn't learn anything of value regarding his whereabouts. However, we now know for sure his car never left Carolina Beach. The car is safely parked in the police lot."

"I'm not concerned about the car, Kevin."

"I know, Anna, but let's divert our thinking to other matters, like Jason's conviction. You were the key to success. It's what we expected for the congressman, Anna. The guy was guilty as sin, and you proved it. He was a sucker for beauty, we all know."

"I'm not comfortable with being a femme fatale, Kevin. He was a monster."

"True, but without meaning to sound patronizing, you are a strikingly attractive woman the poor guy couldn't resist."

Anna emitted a slight laugh. "He wasn't poor before we met. He actually enjoyed a pretty luxurious life style, like his apartment at the Watergate."

Ryan returned the laugh. "You sure changed his life style. Any decision on the contents of the bank box?"

"They're still deliberating the legal issues, Kevin.

I'm not spending the possible payout."

"No, you're too disciplined, Anna, but a rather lucky lady who just might be declared the rightful beneficiary of several million dollars."

"I'd rather have my luck transferred to Del. Are there any new possibilities?"

"In fact, there are," Ryan replied, proceeding to inform Anna of the surprise encounter with Andy Dutton and his extended family. "They are gung-ho to join the search."

"Are those two Russian women in the group?"

"Yes, Natalie and Tanya, along with the housekeeper, Olga. And Rambo, as well."

"I'm not concerned about Olga and Rambo," Anna said with a hint of apprehension, "but those two?"

"The more people looking for Del, the better, in my view, and those ladies are relentless in their pursuits."

"I know, Kevin. I'll be down there tomorrow."

## Chapter Eleven

BALD HEAD ISLAND

Randy King placed his glass of Johnnie Walker Blue on the cocktail table and turned to Montez. "It is time for my daily contact, which I invite you to share with me as my trusted lieutenant."

"I'm honored, Commander."

"Come," King said, rising to lead the way along a long corridor to a locked door. "Watch this," he continued as he faced an eye-level box adjoining a sturdy appearing door. After staring at the box for several seconds, a click was heard and the door opened. "Impressed?" he asked as the pair passed through the door that closed with a solid clunk. "Eye imaging," he continued. "State of the art. The little gem reads my irises—only mine. No one else enters without me."

"I am truly impressed, Commander," Montez said as his eyes traveled over an array of sophisticated looking electronics. "You appear to be very well equipped."

King smiled. "Best Navy money could buy. I didn't leave without some valuable souvenirs."

"Seems fair to me," Montez said, returning King's smile.

King glanced at his wristwatch. "Almost time," he said, energizing a small radio transmitter on a nearby table. He flipped a toggle switch, adjusted a dial, placed the unit on speaker and spoke one word, "Report!" Seconds later, an accented voice responded, "On course!" followed by a distinct click.

King switched off the device and looked at Montez.

"The shipment is well underway. We will soon be able to bring relief to our anxious customers, and several million dollars to our pockets," he added with a beaming smile. "Doesn't it give you a warm feeling to help the needy?"

* * *

"His dream must be over," Malone said in their nearby cottage, as she peered into the adjoining den. "The blanket has receded."

"Wonder what he was dreaming," Daly said with a grin. "If we knew, we might be able to stir his recollection."

"Yeah, something seems to stimulate him," Malone laughed. "What can we do to penetrate his fog?"

"It is frustrating. I often take out my frustrations by playing the piano."

"Hey, maybe that's an approach. I always enjoy hearing you play. Why don't you bang away?"

"Worth a try, Jenny. Should I wait till he awakes?"

"No, maybe he'll think it's the pearly gates calling. Let's see his reaction. Go at it."

Patriotic tunes soon flowed through the cottage, as Daly got into the mood.

"He's awake," Malone reported, "and smiling. I'll talk with him while you play," she added, moving to a chair next to Del's daybed.

"We thought you'd enjoy a little music, and that it might stoke your memory," she addressed their guest. "Do you like music?"

"Sounds good," Del replied, tapping his fingers.

"Any of the tunes sound familiar?" Malone probed.

Del shook his head. "No, sorry."

"You seemed to be dreaming," Malone said. "Do you remember anything about your dreams?"

Del appeared to be staring into space before replying. "Pretty fuzzy. Lots of people running around."

"Men and women?"

Del paused, then shrugged. "Can't remember."

Daly's music then switched to nursery rhymes, and Malone began singing the words of an old favorite:

> *The farmer in the dell*
> *The farmer in the dell*
> *Hi-ho, the derry-o*
> *The farmer in the dell*

As the ditty progressed, Del sat forward with widening eyes. "Dell", he muttered.

"Dell!" Malone repeated. "Is that your name? What does it mean to you?"

"I don't know," Del said, slumping back on his bed.

"That's a start," Malone called to Daly in the next room. "He recognized the word dell. Keep playing."

"We might be getting somewhere," Daly replied in an encouraging voice. "Let's explore the Y on his T-shirt with the Whiffenpoof Song," she said, seguing into the old ballad as Malone sang the words,

> *To the tables down at Mory's*
> *To the place where Louie dwells*
> *To the dear old Temple bar we love so well*
> *Sing the Whiffenpoofs assembled*
> *with their glasses raised on high*

*And the magic of their singing casts its spell*

"His eyes are fluttering, and he seems to be mouthing the words, Leigh. I think we're getting through!"

While the women basked in hopeful discovery, Del lay back. "My headache is returning. Do you have any more Tylenol?" he asked before falling back asleep.

"We're on the brink," Daly declared to her companion. "He recognizes a connection to Yale, and the word dell. Might be time to pass our find on to the authorities."

"I do believe it was your piano pounding that did the trick, Leigh."

"Do I get a music award?" Daly said with a laugh.

"Probably not, but perhaps a Steinway endorsement."

"I was playing on a Yamaha."

"Oh well, so much for that. What do we do now?"

"Make one last try in the morning, then make the call," Daly conceded. "Keep an eye on him, and give him another Tylenol when he wakes up. Do you think he will dream again?"

"I'll keep an eye on the blanket," Malone said with a smile.

* * *

"You are good cooks," Del complimented the next morning, seated at the dining room table with his two hosts, and finishing a western omelet.

"We're pleased that you feel strong enough to get out of that bed," Jenny said, spreading strawberry jam on a croissant.

"I feel quite rested, and my headache is gone. Tell me again how you found me."

Del listened intently as Leigh and Jenny related their discovery, and the struggle to bring him into the cottage.

"I owe you my life," Del said with an appreciative look. "Sure wish I could help figure out who I am. Y doesn't sound too exciting."

"You have given us some leads," Daly said. "You mumbled the words Ann, or and, as well as responding to the word dell and Yale's Whiffenpoof song. We think we're on the verge of breaking into your memory bank. Do you mind us trying to explore?"

"Lord, no, I'm more than happy to answer any questions, and I really enjoyed the music."

Daly beamed. "I didn't destroy your hearing?"

"Absolutely not. It was soothing, and somehow familiar."

"Well, why not try some more, then," Daly said, moving to the corner piano and unlimbering her fingers with a short series of exercises. "How about this," she continued, again playing the Whiffenpoof song, with strong emphasis on the last verse:

> *Gentlemen songsters off on a spree*
> *Doomed from here to eternity*
> *Lord have mercy on such as we*
> *Baa, baa, baa.*

As the last notes lingered, a broad smile engulfed Del's face, and he repeated "Baa, baa, baa."

"That has to be it!" Daly exclaimed. "Dell from Yale! Let's pass that on to the authorities. Let them figure it out. Who do we call? Is there a cop of some kind on the island?"

Malone shrugged. "Don't know. Maybe call 911?"

"Isn't that for emergencies, Jenny? This doesn't quite fit the bill. I saw a sticker near the phone with a number on it. Think I'll try that."

## Chapter Twelve

CAROLINA BEACH

"We got company," Beau Chamberlin called out to Rufus Reynolds who was tinkering with the steering cables of the *Lucky Lady*.

Reynolds looked past his cousin who had been semi-dozing in the sun, and studied the two men approaching on the nearby dock. "Don't tell them anything. Play dumb," Reynolds ordered, thinking to himself that would not be difficult for Beau.

"You've been hard to find," Sheriff Lyle Lawson greeted. "You haven't been around Captain Bill's the several times we checked there."

"Don't spend much time in such establishments," Reynolds replied. "What do you want to see us about?"

"Okay if we come aboard?" Lawson asked. "You've met Special Agent Ryan before."

"Hear he broke some furniture at Captain Bill's," Chamberlin interjected. "We don't want no damage to our boat. Where's the other guy?"

"The other guy is out investigating other crimes, and don't worry, we're just here to ask some questions."

"What do you want to know? We've been busy taking people out fishing. Have to make a living, you know," Reynolds said.

"Dock logs don't show many fishing trips, Rufus."

"Invading our privacy again?"

"Public records, Rufus. You heard about Wanda?"

"Yeah, too bad. She must have hooked up with the

wrong john."

"Any idea who it could be?"

"Not a clue. We was out of town on business."

Lawson signaled a "watch the reaction" look at Ryan, before saying, "Right, someone reported seeing your vans in Southport."

Reynolds tensed. "Any law against going to Southport?"

"No, just saying. You must like Ramon's seafood."

"He buys from us," Reynolds retorted. "Lots of fishermen sell to him. That illegal?"

"Of course not, just don't speed on the way."

"We watch out for the fuzz," Chamberlin interjected, drawing a sharp "keep quiet" glance from Reynolds.

"We're still looking for our missing friend," Ryan said. "Do you have any information about him?"

"Not a peep," Reynolds replied, reaching into a Styrofoam cooler and extracting a can of Colt 45. "Want one?" he asked while effortlessly popping the tab.

"Thanks anyway," Lawson said, followed by Ryan's declination.

"We just want to remind you both," Ryan said, "that it's a serious crime to assault or otherwise harm a Federal law enforcement officer. The penalty could be up to death."

Beau Chamberlin shifted uneasily in his deck chair. "We dint hurt nobody."

"Let us know when you want to go fishing," Reynolds spoke up. "Give you a reduced rate to show our respect for your noble profession."

"We'll be in touch," Ryan said, rising to leave and

addressing Reynolds. "You might want to put something on those scratches to keep them from developing an infection."

Reynolds touched his neck. "Yeah, a good idea," he responded after a brief hesitation. "Scraped it on a bulkhead."

"Oh," Ryan added, "I might take you up on your beer offer if it still holds. Might get thirsty on the trip back."

"Uh, sure," Reynolds stammered, opening the cooler and handing a can to Ryan. "Nothing too good for our brave public servants. You, too sheriff?"

"No, one should be enough, but thanks anyway," Lawson replied.

Ryan watched Reynolds drain his beer can and toss the crushed empty into a nearby overflowing trash bag. "Can I take your trash ashore?" he offered.

"Yeah, why not," Reynolds replied. "It's always a pain getting rid of the crap."

"Just another public service," Ryan said with a smile, picking up the bag.

* * *

"Still lying their butts off," Lawson said as they drove off in the sheriff's cruiser.

"Yeah, Lyle, and did you notice how easily he crushed that can? Strong hands."

"Right, and I caught his reaction when you mentioned his scratches."

Ryan nodded. "There might be some interesting DNA. Remember the item in the M.E.'s report—minute specks of flesh under Wanda's fingernails?"

"Sure do, you rascal you," Lawson said with a knowing smile. "We needed Reynolds DNA and you have his prints, too. Good work."

"All in a day's work," Ryan replied with a satisfied smile as he wrapped his handkerchief around the can handed to him by Reynolds and sorted through Reynold's trash.

\* \* \*

"They're on to us!" Beau Chamberlin moaned with alarm to his cousin. "All those questions about the missing guy, Ramon's, Southport, and Wanda. And the death penalty! We outta get out of town."

"Beau, ya gotta keep calm. That's how they operate—try to scare the shit outta people. We got nothing to worry about if we don't panic."

"Well, they got me worried. Makes me feel like I wanta crap all the time."

"I tell ya not to worry. Think about the dough we'll get when the next shipment arrives. Then we'll have enough money to go hide out anywhere we want."

"You make it sound simple, Rufus, and ya gave away one of the beers I was planning to drink."

"Think about it as bread cast upon the water, Beau. I read that in a magazine once. Cool saying, huh? That little beer investment just might get them off our backs. I'd say it was a pretty clever move."

## Chapter Thirteen

BALD HEAD ISLAND

"Hey, Jenny, guess what I found when I started to call? The sticker by the phone I mentioned earlier is for the Bald Head Island Public Service Department, which includes police. Didn't know they had a police department here."

"Me neither, Leigh. We probably should have called them when we first found Y."

"Well, better late than never. Make the call."

"Got a recording," Daly advised a minute later. "Said the Chief was out on patrol and leave a number. If it's an emergency, call 911."

"So, we finally have things in motion, Leigh. Meanwhile, we need some groceries. Y is demonstrating a growing appetite."

"Yes, time to visit some of those cute stores at the marina. Do we all go?"

"Hmm," Malone replied, "might look weird to have two women carting around a strange man who doesn't know who he is. We might get arrested for adult abduction. Wouldn't that be a hoot? We might make the cover of *The National Enquirer*. I'm sure our families would be thrilled."

"Better if one of us goes, Jenny, and one stays with Y. Toss for it?"

"Heads," Malone declared before the quarter landed on the kitchen table. "Tails. You go."

"Sure you'll feel safe being alone with a big muscular hunk with stimulating dreams?"

Malone grinned. "Someone's got to do it. Let's make up your shopping list."

## SOUTHPORT, NORTH CAROLINA

"Nice looking boat," Andy Dutton said to his extended family as they prepared to board the *RANGER*, the eleven a.m. ferry to Bald Head Island.

"It looks much better than that raft we rode on the Potomac River," Nadia Rostov remarked with a shiver.

"Definitely," Tanya Tamarof agreed, recalling their hair-raising rescue a few months before when they almost plunged into the Great Falls, Virginia, rocks. "It doesn't look like we'll need our heroic rescuer on this voyage," she added, referring to Del Dickerson who had saved the day in the FBI special code-name SPY-TRAP. "And now he's missing. Wonder where he is and what he's doing?"

Olga Servadova smiled broadly as she surveyed the area. "Such fun to go on ferry boat," she said. "I so lucky to be with you."

"It's our good fortune," Lydia Dutton assured. "And, we're looking forward to your delicious meals at the rental cottage."

"I make a seafood goulash," Olga beamed.

"Where is the cottage?" Nadia asked Dutton.

"Only a mile or so from the ferry landing. We need to use an electric cart to get there. I've reserved a big one for us. There are no cars allowed on the island."

"Think Rambo will get seasick ?" Tanya wondered.

Dutton smiled and rubbed his dog's head. " He's a

Lab. Water's his element. Just have to keep him away from the alligators."

"Alligators!" Lydia Dutton exclaimed. "You thinking of disposing of your faithful old wife on this trip?"

"Only if she misbehaves," Dutton responded as the relaxed group boarded the ferry.

Olga had the last word. "I make a mean alligator goulash."

## BALD HEAD ISLAND

Leigh Daly's shopping expedition was highly satisfying. Basic foods and juices, plus a selection of tempting confections, some fresh-caught seafood, and a few bottles of select wine filled her sacks. Life is looking promising, she thought as she loaded her purchases into her cart. As she started to drive away, she had to brake hard to avoid colliding with a large passing cart loaded with people and a large black dog. "Tourists!" she murmured, then smiled, remembering she was one too, but not before beeping her horn at the driver who waved in an apologetic manner. She waved back. No harm done, and we're all here to enjoy the tranquility, so relax girl, she told herself. Moving onto the asphalt cart path, a gnawing sense grew in her mind that the driver looked somehow familiar. She speeded up to get a better look, but before she could overtake the other cart it had turned off on an interesting path. Oh, well, she thought, lots of people look alike. Let's see how things went at the cottage.

"Your color is returning quite well," Jenny Malone told their mystery guest. "It could be a healing sign.

We're doing our best to bring you out of your concussion, or whatever it is. You responded to the words dell, Ann, and baa, baa. We might be getting close to a breakthrough. Should we hit you on the head again?"

Del grimaced. "No, thanks. The headache is just fading away. But I'm so thankful for you two ladies. I'm a lucky guy to be rescued by such lovely, caring women."

Malone waved off the compliment. "Your wife or girlfriend must be frantic in searching for you. Do you recall having either one?"

Del shook his head. "No, but I hope she's as pretty as you and your friend. Where is she?"

Malone suppressed a blush. "You know how to flatter a girl. My friend is out shopping for groceries. We have to feed you to restore your strength."

"I'm feeling pretty strong," Del said. "So, we're by ourselves?"

"Right. Are you worried about being alone with a strange lady?"

"You don't seem like a strange lady. You're more like a guardian angel."

"Do you believe in angels, Y?"

Del nodded. "I think so, but things are getting fuzzy again. I suddenly feel sleepy."

"I'll let you rest, then," Malone said. "It'll give me time to shower before Leigh returns."

Fifteen minutes later, Malone was emerging from a soothing shower when she heard the house phone ringing. Wrapping a towel around her dripping body, she reached the kitchen wall phone just as it stopped ringing. A recorded male voice said it was the Bald Head

Island Police Department returning a call. "Please call back," it ended.

As Malone replaced the handset, she heard a thud in the adjoining den and rushed to investigate, finding Del sprawled on the floor, looking up with a dazed expression. His blanket aside, his shorts displayed distinct elevation. As she hurried to his side, her towel came undone and fell away, leaving her crouching naked over the dormant man at the same time a door slammed. A minute later Daly entered into the room.

"What in the world is going on!" Daly managed to gasp.

"I fell out of bed," Del said. "I think I was dreaming."

"I was trying to help him," Malone said with a flushed face.

"I need a drink," Daly said, handing Malone her towel and sagging into a nearby chair.

## Chapter Fourteen

CAROLINA BEACH

"Anything new?" Anna Chen asked Kevin Ryan when they met in the Hampton Inn lobby. "I've prayed the whole way from Washington."

Ryan hugged the strikingly attractive woman and shook his head in a futile gesture. "Let's assume that no news means good news. My gut tells me we'll get a break any minute."

"Ever the optimist," Chen said with a wan smile. "You always cheer me up. Is there anything left undone?"

"Not here, Anna. We're waiting on the DNA results on the woman's murder, hoping it will provide leverage on the two no-goods from the bar where Del disappeared, Captain Bill's. Meanwhile, we have a group of eager-beaver hunters an hour south of here, just chomping on the bit to do something."

"You mean Mr. Dutton, and those Russian women."

"Yeah, plus Rambo, Mrs. Dutton and Olga. They're on Bald Head Island. Perhaps we should join them and share ideas while we wait."

Chen shrugged. "Funny name. Guess it's better than worrying here. Isn't there an old saying that misery loves company?"

"An old one, Anna, and I have a Chinese saying for you: 'Fortune blesses those who hope.'"

Chen looked confused. "Not Confucius, I believe."

Ryan laughed. "Right. Came from a fortune cookie

slip printed in New York City."

"You are a bright light in my life," Chen said with a laugh. "I don't know what I would do without your support."

"I'm here for you and Del, Anna. I know quality, and it's tradition to not leave a comrade behind. I'm committed to finding our missing link. Besides, he owes me a beer."

"Well that's certainly enough to keep you interested," Chen said, stretching to impart a warm kiss on Ryan's lips. "You're a good man, and I'm forever indebted."

Maybe I shouldn't try so hard to find my buddy, was Ryan's fleeting thought as he savored the sensation of Anna Chen's stimulating kiss.

Refocusing, Ryan suggested, "Why don't we leave your car in the sheriff's secure lot here and drive to Southport together? That's where we catch the ferry to the Island."

"Sounds like a plan to me," Chen replied. "How do you like my American saying?"

"Great, Anna. I do believe you have captured the essence of today's American culture."

"You're a dear," she said, squeezing his arm. "I feel so secure in your hands. Shall we proceed?"

As they drove south on North Carolina Highway 87, with a few of Del's belongings secured in his trunk, Ryan mentally retrieved what data he knew about his exotic companion. Sponsored into the United States by a powerful Senator on promises of finding her American Army father who had left his fiancée in Taiwan, unaware of her pregnancy, Anna had been obscenely exploited by the married legislator, who established her in a luxury Georgetown townhouse. That's where she met Del, who was investigating the unscrupulous senator's fraudulent schemes. A violent auto accident, while the senator was fleeing from apprehension, ended his life and severely injured Anna, who was tenderly cared for by Del during her recuperation. A robust romance flourished, accompanied by their subsequent involvement in a number of colorful FBI cases, and oft-deferred matrimonial plans.

Glancing at the beautiful woman with an intriguing blend of oriental and occidental features, Ryan saw her nodding in drowsiness as the car sped along in light traffic. You have much to live for, Del. Let's pray for another dose of your famous good luck. I have my fingers crossed.

## BALD HEAD ISLAND

"You don't really think I was trying to seduce him, do you?" Malone sputtered as she addressed Daly and tightened the knot on her terry towel.

Daly suppressed a grin. "Well, it sure didn't look good."

"What! You still think I ... Come on, Leigh, you know me better than that."

"Gee. I don't know, Jenny. He is a rather attractive specimen. Everyone has a breaking point."

"Unbelievable! You honestly think I was trying something?"

Daly couldn't contain her laughter longer. "Relax, Jenny, just teasing. I have the utmost confidence in your integrity," Daly concluded with a laugh.

"Ahem," Del sounded from the floor, displaying a broad smile. "I just want to say that I didn't feel threatened, but admit it was quite a stimulating sight."

Malone's face reddened further. "I'm going to get dressed," she declared, heading out of the room. "Don't take advantage of the 'attractive specimen' while I'm gone," Malone told Daly with a meaningful wink.

Turning to Del, with an impish grin, Daly said, "Hope you don't mind a little girl jousting. You've given us a diversion from our daily routines."

"Go for it," Del responded, moving into a chair. "I'm at your disposal."

"Hopefully, we might soon learn who you are," Daly advised. "I'm trying to reach the island police department. We just found out that they have one here, and probably should have called them when we found you. We're just visitors here. The lady who owns this cottage would have known what to do. Anyway, we might be able to finally learn who you are, and stop calling you Y."

"I'm really sorry for all the trouble I've caused you nice ladies."

"No need to apologize. We are happy to help, and, frankly, it's been rather enjoyable. Why are you grimacing?" Daly suddenly asked with alarm. "Are you in pain?"

Del nodded. "A little. I must have banged something when I fell out of bed," he said, grasping his left upper thigh.

"I'm a nurse," Daly said. "I can check for you if you-would like for me to.

Del nodded again. "If you don't mind."

"It's what we do," Daly said. "Drop your pants."

"Hmm, red and a bit swollen," Daly was saying as she examined the area at the same time Malone returned.

Malone chuckled with a broad smile. "Inspecting the 'attractive specimen', I see."

Daly raised her hands in a surrender gesture. "Okay. We're even. Should we move on?"

"Agreed," Malone said, "and I have an idea. Let's call Yale and see if they can identify Dell or Del from Yale."

"Quite a long shot, Jenny, but why not? Give it a whirl."

"I'll ask the Registrar to see what their computers can come up with, giving estimated graduation dates based on our guess of his approximate age."

"Nothing ventured, nothing gained," Daly said. "Go for it."

"Another of your favorite bromides, Leigh. Let's hope it works."

\* \* \*

"Welcome to paradise," Andy Dutton greeted Anna Chen and Kevin Ryan as they debarked the 11 a.m. ferry from Southport. "You look wonderful," he told the striking woman, "and you haven't deteriorated much since last week," he said to Ryan. "Good trip?"

"Lovely countryside and a smooth boat ride," Chen remarked.

Ryan scanned the broad confluence of water where

*Old Baldy* - S H Williams

the Cape Fear River meets the Atlantic Ocean. "Much larger than the maps indicate. I'm impressed."

"It's part of the Intracoastal Waterway," Dutton noted.

"A most intriguing area," Ryan said, "especially *Old Baldy*, North Carolina's oldest standing lighthouse. You can see it standing proudly near the harbor," he continued, pointing at the sand-colored structure. "We can climb to the top while we're here. It provides quite a view of the surroundings."

"It's beautiful," Anna said. "You're a fount of information, Kevin, how do you know so much?"

Ryan smiled. "I read a lot of the tourist literature. Also," he added with a fleeting, far-away gaze, "lighthouses bring back special memories. They were a SEAL's best friend on occasion when our team was approaching an unfriendly foreign shore."

"Oh, of course," Chen responded, "you were a Navy SEAL. I imagine you have a host of exciting stories to tell."

"Or, not to tell," Ryan replied with a wistful look. "That was another day. Let's concentrate our attention now on finding our elusive friend."

"I agree, Kevin. Maybe he's hiding in a lighthouse somewhere."

"That's the optimistic spirit, Anna. Who knows where he might turn up."

"And wait till you see the rest of the island," Dutton interjected. "The remainder of my gang is lolling on the beach close to the cottage. Let's have lunch before we join them. We're right near *Mojo's*, said to have great seafood. We can update each other on our search for Del."

"Not much new," Ryan said as they were seated at an outside table overlooking a glistening harbor filled with luxury yachts. "We're still waiting for the DNA results on Rufus in the murder of the Captain Bill's waitress. Del's car was found near the charter boat dock, so we know he didn't leave town in it. All we need is one of his miraculous appearances."

"Oh, I dearly pray so," Chen sighed, looking imploringly at Dutton whose eyes were following a couple that was being seated at a nearby table.

"Guy looks familiar," Dutton said, straining to get a better look.

As the new arrival turned to accept a menu from an attentive young waitress, his eyes met Dutton's and flashed a sign of recognition.

The trim, middle-aged man with close-cropped silver hair rose and approached, broadcasting a broad, bright smile. "Andy Dutton?" he asked. "If you're not, you have a double."

"Chuck Phillips?" Dutton replied, jumping to his feet. "Haven't seen you since we worked some cases together in Virginia. Still with Customs?"

"Retired two years, Andy. Touring the country with my wife. How about you? Still toiling for the FBI?"

"About to retire, Chuck. I'm here with extended family for an adjustment vacation," he said, pausing to introduce Chen and Ryan. "We have a rental cottage for a week. You?"

"We booked a room at the *Marsh Harbour Inn* for a few days. Maybe we'll see you on the beach. Hope you have a relaxing stay."

"That was the plan, Chuck, until we learned that one of our prized agents, who happens to be Anna's fiancé, mysteriously disappeared after a fishing outing with Kevin at Carolina Beach. That's about an hour north of here." Dutton and Ryan provided a brief summary. "You can imagine our intense personal concern," Dutton concluded.

"For sure," Phillips said. "Good luck in your search, and let me know if I can help in any way. I still have some contacts with my old Customs associates," he said, presenting his business card before returning to his table.

"A good guy," Dutton told Ryan and Chen, "and an excellent investigator. Handled a lot of smuggling cases, including drugs. Who knows what will unravel this puzzle," he said, pocketing Phillips' card. "Maybe we can put him back to work."

## Chapter Fifteen

"A great intro lunch," Ryan proclaimed as they left *Mojo's on the Harbor* and climbed into the six-passenger electric cart that came with the rental cottage.

"Attach the seat belts," Dutton said from behind the wheel. "This is bigger than the golf carts at the club back home, and they're lots more of them flitting around. Don't want anyone falling out from an inadvertent bump."

"You're right there," Ryan agreed as they dodged dozens of similar carts while following the asphalt road to the rental cottage. There they found the rest of their party that was returning from the beach, thirsty and hungry.

Chen and Ryan were warmly welcomed. Rambo's overt affection seemingly more enthusiastic than that of Nadia Rostov who was semi-clothed in a lace cover up that minimally covered the red string-bikini that barely encased her provocative figure.

"Nice to see you again," Rostov said. "We are all distressed about Del, and hoping for some good news. We all know he's a survivor."

"Yes," Chen agreed. He survived you, was her uncharitable thought. "We are all praying for some of his legendary luck," she said.

"We found a beautiful secluded portion of the beach," Tamarof said to Anna Chen. "A wonderful place to expose our bodies to the healing sun without prying eyes. You should join us after lunch."

"I do want to enjoy the beach," Chen replied.

"First, we eat," the booming voice of Olga Servadova announced from the kitchen where a plate of sandwiches suddenly appeared. "I like cook job. Goulash later."

* * *

"Finally made contact," Daly told Malone. "The Chief is coming over. Said he didn't understand why we hadn't called earlier when I told him we found a man washed up on the beach--one who doesn't know who he is."

"Pardon me if I'm thinking 'told you so.'"

"Yeah, but we decided to try it our way, and didn't realize there was a police department on Bald Head Island."

"Water over the dam," Malone said," if I may borrow one of your favorite quotes."

"You may," Daly said with a friendly nod, turning toward the street at the sound of a car's engine. "Automobile? Didn't think they were allowed."

Minutes later a neatly uniformed policeman carrying an oversize briefcase was knocking on the cottage door. "Miz Daly?" he asked. "I'm Chief Martin. I recognize this place -- belongs to Mrs. Champion, I believe."

"She's my cousin," Malone said from her position behind Daly. "She's coming down soon, but we've been enjoying her hospitality in the meantime."

"Quietly," Daly interjected, "before our discovery." She and Malone delivered brief synopses of their find, and subsequent experience with the stranger. "He's sitting in the den," Daly concluded.

"Well, let's just meet the gent," Martin suggested, following the women.

"Good afternoon," Martin said cordially, extending his hand. "I'm Chief Dennis Martin of the Bald Head Island Police Department. Who are you?"

Del responded with a wry smile. "These nice ladies call me Y."

"Y?" Martin asked the women.

"We think he may have attended Yale," Malone said. "See the big black Y on his T-shirt? He also somewhat responded to the word Dell. I just called the Registrar's office there and asked them to run a computer check on a Dell or Del from Yale. The lady sounded rather skeptical, but said she enjoyed challenges and would make a try."

"Your name Dell or Del?" Martin asked.

Del shrugged. "Wish I knew."

"Well, let's try a little basic investigative procedure," he said, retrieving a small fingerprint kit from his briefcase. "Ever been fingerprinted?"

Del shrugged again. "Don't know. Go ahead."

Chief Martin swiftly imprinted Del's prints on a 5 by 8-inch white card, photographed the entire card with his iPhone, tapped in an address and pushed send. "Off to the FBI's fingerprint division," he remarked. "If you've ever been arrested, served in the military, worked for the government, or been printed for personal identification reasons, they can tell. Might take a little time," he added, "depending on how busy they are."

Daly noticed Del's eyes blink rapidly when Martin mentioned FBI, and brought it to the Chief's attention.

"Might mean something," he said. "Might as well give you the deluxe island treatment while I'm here," Martin said jocularly, "a DNA swab. Any objection?"

Del shook his head. "Okay with me," he said watching Martin unseal a package and extract a cotton tipped stick which he used to collect a saliva sample from the inside of Del's cheek. He placed the saturated swab into an envelope that he sealed and pronounced ready to mail. "This will take a little longer," he declared.

"I'm impressed," Daly said.

"Figured we were a hick department, right?" Martin asked with a smile.

"Well, to be honest, I didn't expect such sophistication," Daly admitted. "My late husband was an FBI agent."

"We received some great training from them," Martin said, "and we have a rather unique department -- all of my officers are cross-trained as police, fire, and medical specialists."

"I heard a car motor," Daly noted.

"Right, there are a few motorized vehicles on the island—police, fire, ambulances, service vehicles. Electric carts wouldn't work in keeping our residents and visitors safe."

"We should have called you right away," Malone volunteered.

"No harm done," Martin replied. "Y looks well cared for. It's understandable you weren't aware as visitors of our facilities that don't get much use midweek and off-season. But, during busy times, you sometimes think of Coney Island. Our little gem is only three miles long, with many marshes, so it can get crowded. By the way, Y looks in good physical condition, like he works our regularly, and has a firm grip. I noticed a slight callous on his right trigger finger when I printed him. Wonder if he might be a cop?"

"Wouldn't that be something?" Daly exclaimed.

"Facts are often stranger than fiction," the chief declared, packing his gear. "I'll be in touch as soon as I hear something. Call me if he suddenly remembers his name," he added, giving each woman his business card. "We're as close as your phone."

* * *

"So what do we do in the meantime?" Malone asked as they waved goodbye to the chief.

"It's another glorious day," Daly observed, "and we're only a few hundred feet from one of the best beaches on the coast. What's logical?"

"Absolutely, Leigh, plus a bit of sunshine might be beneficial to Y—might even jar his memory. Don your suit, grab the sun screen, and let's go."

## Chapter Sixteen

Olga Servadova's eyes brimmed with tears as she gazed open-jawed at the pristine beach that gently sloped into the soft waves of the green-blue Atlantic Ocean. "I am so lucky," she said, dropping a basket of snacks and drinks onto the sand. "God is good."

While the others stretched out beach towels and applied sun block, Nadia Rostov and Tanya Tamarof excused themselves to head for the shielded dune area they had found earlier to enjoy full body exposure. "You're invited to join us, of course," Rostov told Chen and the Duttons with a smile.

"Thanks, anyway," Andy Dutton replied with a grin. "I burn too easily."

"How about you, Anna?" Rostov pursued.

"I believe I'll stay here and watch Rambo chase the birds," Chen answered.

"Watch out for burrs," Olga Servadova warned, plopping down on her towel.

\* \* \*

Less than a half-mile away, Daly, Malone, and Del were relaxing on the same beach.

"This is close to where we found you," Daly said. "Does it stir any memories?"

Del shook his head. "Sorry, but it does look lovely. I'm amazed at how you two wonderful ladies were able to haul my carcass to your cottage. You told me how you used the cart's trailer, and huffed and puffed to get me inside the cottage. I'm more indebted than ever to you, and hope I can repay you someday. It's rather frustrating not to know who you are."

"We're working on that," Malone said. "We might have an answer any day. Aren't you curious?"

"That's for certain. What if I turn out to be a gangster or mad scientist, or something?"

"Or a movie star or astronaut?" Daly speculated.

"You've certainly made our vacation enjoyable," Malone observed. "My cousin, Peggy, the owner of the cottage, has missed all the fun. She's due here later today. Won't she be surprised."

"We seemed to have some recognition when I played Yale's Whiffenpoof song," Daly said. "Should we try it again?"

"Why not?" Del said, "it sounded uplifting," prompting the women to render an enthusiastic, if off-key, rendition.

When they ended, Del shook his head in disappointment. "Thanks for trying," he said. "I do like music," he continued, commencing to whistle a series of patriotic tunes, finishing with *Yankee Doodle Dandy*.

"The last one sounded so good to me, I'll do it over," he said, repeating the tune with raised volume.

* * *

At the Dutton beach site, Rambo, their spirited black Labrador family pet, tired of chasing the elusive surf birds, wandered towards the isolated dune indentation where Nadia Rostov and Tanya Tamarof were absorbing the sun's rays in full European nudity style. Sniffing his way, Rambo was attracted by Rostov's apple-red string bikini and grasped it from the sand with his impressive teeth.

"HEY!" Rostov shouted as Rambo danced playfully away. She grabbed a dangling bit of the glistening fabric, which only encouraged Rambo to pull further away in a seeming game of tug.

"NYET!" Rostov yelled, tugging at the garment and jumping to her feet, prompting Rambo to bound away with the woman's bikini firmly gripped in his jaw. As the dog ran north past the rest of the Dutton party, the group joined the pursuit, Rostov now garbed in the see-through cover up she had quickly donned. Tanya Tamarof, also quickly redressed in her tiny garment, joined the chase. Shouts of "Come back Rambo!" followed the bounding Lab. As soon as the pursuers neared the exuberant canine, he would shake the colorful bikini in his mouth and resume his exciting game.

"Maybe the folks ahead will stop him," Ryan said hopefully, pointing to a cluster of people several yards ahead.

"I think he's tiring of the game," Dutton puffed, watching Rambo pause periodically and look back at his pursuers.

"Sure hope so, Andy. Everyone's getting winded," Ryan was saying when Rambo suddenly stopped with raised ears, then raced towards the strangers who were now within a few hundred feet. Watching wide-eyed, the pursuers were astounded to see Rambo drop the bikini, leap into the arms of a shorts-clad man, and eagerly lick his face.

Approaching closer, Dutton shouted with amazement, "PRAISE THE SAINTS! IT'S DEL! "

## Chapter Seventeen

Pandemonium reigned as Anna Chen hugged her fiancé. Dutton and Ryan pounded his back, Nadia Rostov and Tanya Tamarof hovered nearby possessively, and Lydia Dutton and Olga Servadova beamed brightly. Rambo jumped enthusiastically amidst the celebrants.

"You're alive!" Chen proclaimed with tearing eyes.

"Who are you?" Dutton inquired of Daly and Malone.

They gave their names. "We found him," Daly said. "Who is he? We call him Y."

Dutton shook his head in wonderment. "A guy with incredible good luck. His name is Delbert Dickerson. He's an FBI Agent who disappeared mysteriously from Carolina Beach a few days ago. That's about thirty miles north of here."

"His name is Del!" Malone exclaimed. "Did he happen to attend Yale?"

"Yes, how did you know?"

Malone clapped her hands. "We figured it out. We're natural-born investigators," she said with a beaming smile.

"My late husband was an FBI Agent," Daly said. "Blaine Daly."

"Blaine Daly," Dutton repeated. "A highly respected agent who passed too soon. I worked for him in Washington several years ago. This is almost too much to believe—usually happens only in the movies."

"You said you found him," Ryan asked. "Where?"

"Just a few feet from here," Daly said, pointing to

the waterline. "He was unconscious, and had a big bump on his head. He had apparently just washed up on the shore. There was no one around, so we took him to our cottage. He doesn't know who he is. We've been trying to learn his identity."

"He still seems distant and confused," Dutton acknowledged. "Didn't appear to recognize his fiancée. Let me check," he said, approaching Del who appeared overwhelmed by the jubilant throng surrounding him.

"Do you know who I am?" Dutton asked Del. Del smiled politely. "No, just that you seem to be a pleasant and authoritative man."

"And her?" Dutton asked, nodding towards Chen.

"A very beautiful woman," Del replied.

Anna Chen looked alarmed.

"How about this guy?" Dutton asked, pointing at Ryan.

"An obviously fit man, with a nice smile."

"What about these two women?" Dutton proceeded, nodding towards Rostov and Tamarof.

"Good looking, with great figures."

"How about me?" Olga Servadova interjected. "Do you remember you owe me a pot handle?"

Del grinned. "I think I better repay you," he said to everyone's laughter.

"Apparent amnesia," Daly said. "I saw similar cases when I was nursing. Probably needs a brain specialist."

As the energetic group clustered around Del, Rambo pranced around in the prevailing joyous spirit, reveling in a host of affectionate pats. With his long black tail wagging wildly, the stimulated canine launched another leap towards Del's arms. Caught off balance, Del lurched against Nadia Rostov, knocking her to the sand where she sprawled wide-eyed on her back, her flimsy gown gathered around her neck. Unable to retain his footing, Del pitched forward, bouncing his head against Malone's sturdy plastic cooler before landing atop Nadia, his face cradled between her thighs in a position that could be interpreted as obscene.

Panicky screams filled the air, as Ryan and Dutton sprang to assist, rolling Del off the startled woman.

"Good Lord!" Anna Chen yelled, hurrying to aid Del whose eyes were tightly closed. "What next?" she implored, watching Ryan position himself to begin CPR, as the others hovered over the dormant man in disbelief.

"Look!" Nadia shouted seconds later, "his eyelids are fluttering."

Suddenly, Del's eyes opened, and he looked around in bewilderment. "Anna!" was his first word.

His eyes continued to scan the group. "Nadia! Tanya! Mr. and Mrs. Dutton! Kevin! Olga! Rambo! What's going on? Where are we? What are you all doing here?"

"Looking for you," Dutton declared to a round of cheers.

Rambo lunged forward to lick Del's face.

"My prayers were answered," Anna Chen cried, hugging Del.

"We have a lot to clarify," Dutton said.

"Why don't we all go to our cottage?" Malone suggested. "It's just a short distance from here."

"I have a headache," Del said, looking at Ryan. "Weren't we supposed to have dinner tonight?"

Ryan smiled. "You've been on a little trip, buddy. We all need to sit down and talk about it."

"A gift from God," Olga said. "I'll cook a celebration dinner."

"And I'll provide the wine," Daly volunteered.

"What a blessed day," Chen said, caressing Del's head. "Your fortunate luck came through once more."

"You are my good luck, Anna," Del said, implanting a tender kiss.

Turning to Ryan, Del said, "Something went haywire after we had a beer in that joint near the dock."

"That's for sure," Ryan confirmed. "We've been checking it out—there's something rotten there. The waitress who served us was murdered."

"The red head?" Del asked. "That's awful. She was rather provocative, but nice."

"That's her. Or was her. She was strangled after we started asking questions about your disappearance. She contacted us and wanted to talk. Her body was dumped in an adjoining town. What do you remember before just coming to?"

"The last thing I remember," Del said, with Dutton listening attentively, "was entering a back room after going to the john that had a funny name. I saw two guys sitting at a table sorting baggies."

"Drugs?"

"Sure looked like it to me, which was why I asked them what they were doing. Wrong question, I guess, since one of the guys asked what I hell I was doing there. The other guy jumped up, grabbing a beer bottle. That's the last I recall. The lights must have gone out immediately."

"It's understandable you don't remember anything more," Ryan said. "We've been trying to reconstruct what happened to you next. How you got into the ocean and washed up on Bald Head Island. It's nothing short of wondrous. By the way, a trash man found your badge," he continued, pulling it from his pocket and handing it to Del. "I have your other property in my bag – creds, gun, cell phone."

"Great," Del said, smiling brightly. "I don't feel quite as naked now. My wonderful rescuers told me they found nothing in my pockets. Had about seventy bucks, best I can estimate. Also, my wristwatch is missing."

"We've made some progress, Del, and now we'll be looking for some dude wearing your Rolex."

"Better known as a Timex Ironman," Del chuckled, "but I'll recognize it. It has Anna's name engraved on the back."

## Chapter Eighteen

Peggy Champion's cottage was jumping with celebratory occupants when she drove up in the personal electric cart she maintained at the ferry harbor. "What's going on?" she asked her cousin after quickly stashing her mild-mannered golden cocker spaniel "Buddy" in a side screened porch. "Whatever is happening, you seem to be enjoying the place."

Malone glowed. "Oh, Peggy, wait till you hear what's occurred. Your place will be famous."

"Or infamous?" Champion ventured with a worried look as she carried her suitcase into her previously sedate residence. Malone followed with two loaded grocery bags and introduced the unexpected guests. "We just met on the beach," she explained "and they all know Y, who we just learned is Del Dickerson. You won't believe what's transpired."

"Try me," Champion said, displaying her poise as an accomplished artist who studied people and events as wife of a State Department diplomat.

Malone began her explanation. "Well, I told you on the phone that we found a mysterious man on the beach."

"And I suggested you call 911."

"Right," Malone conceded, "but we thought we could bring him out of his amnesia with our efforts."

"Didn't work, right, Jenny?"

"Correct, but we finally learned who he is."

"A drug smuggler? We've had some of them on the island before."

"No, an FBI Agent! Apparently dumped into the

ocean up north around Carolina Beach. Somehow, he floated down to where we found him."

"He's one lucky man," Champion observed.

"Mr. Dutton and Mr. Ryan are both FBI Agents, it turns out, and they are quizzing him about the circumstances. It's exciting."

"I'm anxious to hear more, Jenny. Glad your visit wasn't boring."

"Stay tuned," Malone said, answering her ringing iPhone. "It's the Bald Head Island Police Chief."

"An old friend," Champion noted. "Find out what he has to say."

Miller listened attentively to Chief Martin. "Delbert Dickerson," she repeated aloud, "a missing FBI agent. Thank you so much, Chief. Your tried and true techniques paid off, and I must be honest, since you've been so helpful, but we just learned that on the beach. His memory abruptly returned when he was knocked down and bumped his head again."

"Well, to be completely honest with you, Miz Malone, I just received a BOLO on a missing person notice filed in our adjoining jurisdiction, New Hanover County. It said your mystery guest has been found and identified. So, we're even, and everyone is happy. The old methods worked, and justice has been served. Let me know if I can be of further help."

Malone had just rung off when her phone chirped again. "Yale University," she said, recognizing the incoming phone number. Connecting, she listened with a growing expression of satisfaction before terminating with profuse expressions of thanks.

"When it rains, it pours," she quoted. "It was the

Yale Registrar. She said, despite her misgivings, that they found 'Del from Yale,' matching our age estimates with possible graduation years, and found a graduate named Delbert G. Dickerson. Their records listed him as becoming an FBI agent, last address shown as San Francisco. I thanked her and promised to sing the Whiffenpoof song at every opportunity. So, what comes next?"

"Set up one of our bedrooms for Del and Anna," Champion instructed. "They deserve rest and a little privacy."

"Isn't she something?" Malone asked Daly, watching her cousin graciously welcoming her new guests.

Daly grinned. "Indeed. We've seen her in action and shared some great times together," she said, glancing in the direction of Champion who had begun unloading her groceries. "She stays in great shape-- looks more like forty than AARP eligible. Remember the laughs when a rookie waitress cards us on girl's night out?"

"Smart young server," Malone noted. "Generates a healthy tip."

"And her youthful spirit often inspires male patrons to send drinks our way," Daly said with a chuckle, "especially when an alcoholic haze engulfs an establishment."

Their reflections were interrupted by the subject of their discussion when Peggy Champion gained everyone's attention with the question, "Is anyone besides me hungry?"

"A great idea," Daly said, "and it will give the men the opportunity to discuss business. From my experience as an FBI wife, I know this matter will focus their attention 24/7."

"And I will cook!" Olga Servadova stated, emerging from her examination of the well-equipped kitchen. "It's a dream," she declared. "Seafood now. Goulash another day."

"Settled," Champion announced. "And time for a cocktail."

"Beer and soft drinks in the fridge," Malone said.

"I'll uncork the wine," Daly volunteered.

"Hard stuff in the bar cabinet," Champion concluded before addressing Rambo. "Doggie treats in the kitchen, next to Buddy's dish. He's my traveling partner, waiting to meet you."

Rambo's tail wagged as he followed the trim hostess to the side porch where she hugged her favorite pet. "You have a new friend," she said to Buddy who warily studied the much larger Lab moving slowly forward. Both canines proceeded to sniff and circle about the porch in an apparent sizing-up process. After a minute or so, Rambo stretched out on a mat and yawned, displaying an array of impressive teeth. Buddy cautiously approached, tail wagging, and finally reclined about a foot away from Rambo, snout to snout. Seconds later, Rambo stretched out his right paw towards Buddy. After a brief hesitation, Buddy duplicated the movement, placing his golden paw atop Rambo's. Rambo's tail wagged in a friendly fashion, and be emitted a firm bark. Buddy returned a series of musical chirps.

"Wonderful!" Champion proclaimed, awarding each canine a doggie bone. "Looks like this group will get along beautifully," she said before hurrying away to help Olga select cooking equipment.

Back in the expansive family room, Dutton, Ryan and Del were engaged in discussion. "We obviously have some heavy-duty items to resolve," Dutton noted, "something beyond the attempted murder of Del."

"And an unsolved murder," Ryan pointed out.

Del's voice sounded emphatic. "I'm anxious to see a pair of guys I last saw in a certain Carolina Beach bar."

Overhearing their conversation, Champion contributed a comment. "Welcome to peaceful little Bald Head Island where nothing exciting occurs. I suspect our image is about to change."

*The Old Boathouse* - Mixed Water-Media Painting by Sarah Hasty Williams

## Chapter Nineteen

"Ready for a thrill ride?" Peggy Champion greeted the group waiting at the Dutton cottage the morning after their celebration party.

"You haven't steered us wrong yet, "Andy Dutton responded, "that seafood was out of the world."

"Your cook did it justice," Champion replied. "She's a gem."

"Russia's loss," Dutton said. "Wait till you taste her goulash."

"Nice to see the rest of you again," Champion said to Del, Anna, and Ryan. "No other takers? I have my partner," she continued, pointing to her prized pet resting perkily next to her in a basket strapped to the side of the cart. Buddy's tail wagged at the group smiling his way. "You'll note the red, white, and blue pillow he's sitting on-- a patriotic guy."

"Way to go," Ryan proclaimed.

Dutton reported on the rest of his group. "Lydia and Olga decided to do some cleaning and cooking. Nadia and Tanya are heading back to the beach for some more sun, and Rambo is still sleeping, probably exhausted from chasing that ball around with your Buddy."

"Cute pair," Champion laughed. "Okay, ready to cast off? Strap yourselves in. Woman driver at the wheel."

Dutton took the front passenger seat next to Champion, Del and Anna occupied the second row, and Ryan climbed into the third row. As Champion carefully piloted the cart below the 22-mile-per-hour speed limit along the curving roads, she pointed out points of interest, interspersed with local history. "Originally named Smith Island, after a land-grant owner of the same name, it was later named Bald Head Island, reportedly in recognition of its topographical appearance as a growing sand pile that resembled a bald head. Its unique lighthouse, the oldest still standing lighthouse in North Carolina, was nicknamed 'Old Baldy'. Pardon me if you've heard this before. It's part of my usual tour travelogue. I really enjoy showing my beautiful island to visitors."

"No need to apologize," Chen said. "You do such a wonderful job, and I'm amazed at the lush vegetation -- all the palm trees."

"Yes, we are at the northernmost edge of tropical vegetation, thus all the palm trees and marshes."

"Where I hear alligators dwell," Ryan interjected from his rear seat.

Champion waved at a man in a passing cart. "That's former Senator Billingsworth," she informed. "We have a few retired politicians residing here. Back to other alligators, Kevin," Champion chuckled, "you are correct. They usually stay in the marsh area, but occasionally one takes a stroll and ends up on someone's porch. Quite a shock to the occupant, of course, and you need an expert to remove them. It's illegal to kill them. They're normally not a danger to humans, who manage to keep their distance, but occasionally a wandering dog or cat venturing too close to the marshes disappears."

"Let's not venture too close to the marshes," Anna Chen cautioned.

"There's the path to the beach where you were found," Champion said to Del, pointing in that direction.

"Still wonder how I got there," Del commented.

"We need to solve that mystery," Ryan agreed. "When I talked last night with Sheriff Lawson in Carolina Beach about Del's location he said he'd been asking questions around the dock where Rufus and Beau berth the *Lucky Lady*. He said he had an interview scheduled this morning that might be productive. He didn't elaborate, but promised to keep us posted."

Dutton spoke up. "Now that we know that drugs are involved, we need to expand our horizons. You remember the old Customs colleague we met at the restaurant? Chuck Phillips? He mentioned that he retains contact with his old organization, which just might have some relevant information about drug smuggling in the area."

"Call him," Ryan urged.

"Will do," Dutton agreed, searching his wallet for Phillips' business card.

"Now here's an interesting area," Champion said, turning into a narrow lane bordering a marshland canal. "It's close to the landmark Old Boat House you see located on the island map I provided when we started."

"Very secluded," Ryan remarked. "You can hardly see the cottages through the thick foliage."

"For sure," Champion replied, carefully driving the cart along the metal guardrail. "This is close to a canal that leads to the Cape Fear River and Southport. A smuggler's roadway," she added, continuing their explanatory tour.

\* \* \*

"More curious tourists," Randy King said to his guest after peering through a narrow break in the dense foliage obscuring his cottage from the road.

"You can hardly see your place from the street." Ramon Montez replied from his thickly padded lounge chair on King's screened porch. "My usual canal route on my Sea-Doo avoids such traffic."

"A worthy precaution, Ramon. Just remember to stay on the elevated walkway over the marshes on your way here from my dock. The gators' are always looking for a good meal."

"I move swiftly and alertly, Commander. I was born in the jungle."

"I know, Ramon. It's one reason I have such confidence in you. The authorities are becoming more and more of a nuisance, by the way, hampering hard working businessmen from making a living," King said with a smirk.

Montez smiled in understanding. "Yes, Commander, my rear freezer is almost empty of product."

"It won't be long, my friend. My last contact informed me of our cargo's good progress.

The boat was then not far off Haiti. Our new technology and a tip from an old Navy associate have helped us evade the eyes of the damned Coast Guard hounds who have become a major irritant. But the new boat has what it takes to outsmart their efforts, so our patience should pay off handsomely within a few days. I trust your courier chain is ready to perform properly."

"Yes, they are ready to offload the cargo and transport it here. They've been lying low in the meantime."

"Excellent, it would not be healthy for any of us if their behavior attracted undue attention. You feel confident in them?"

Montez gulped before replying, recalling he had not heard from Rufus and Beau for several days. "Absolutely," he answered with emphasis. "I'll be in touch with them tomorrow."

Where are the bastards, he wondered.

\* \* \*

"Well, now that you've seen the Shoals Club," Champion said after a visit to the historic club, "we might like to head back for lunch."

"'Olga said she was preparing her famous goulash," Dutton informed. "We sure don't want to miss that."

"That's a beautiful club," Chen remarked about the rambling Shoals Club overlooking a line of partially submerged sand bars.

"It's aptly named, Anna. The shoals out there are a popular place for people to watch the setting sun. They walk out on the shoals while they're above water at low tide. Only problem," she said with a chuckle, "some folks occasionally get stuck out there when the tide comes in and they hadn't returned to shore in time."

"Oh, my, do any of them drown?" Chen wondered.

"No. Fortunately, the island has a very active volunteer rescue team in-season when the unwary risk disaster, so I haven't heard of anyone being lost. Several returned with wet feet and soggy pant legs, however. Most of us respect the powers of nature."

"Nothing to fool with," Del volunteered. "And it can

be fickle--like delivering me to this heavenly beach."

"Nature and divine intervention," Dutton observed.

"Amen," Chen agreed. "Someone up there is looking out for its little black sheep."

"Baa, baa, baa," Del contributed to everyone's laughter.

"So," Champion said, "you've had my nutshell tour of Bald Head Island. Hope you enjoyed it."

Expressions of thanks emerged from her passengers as she steered her cart into a narrow lane that ended in a cul-de-sac bordered by a steel guard rail anchored into the edge of the asphalt. Immediately behind the guardrail was a thick marsh, covered with a murky film of water glistening about a foot below the pavement surface.

"Wrong turn," Champion was saying when two young bicyclists darted from nowhere directly in front of the cart. Reacting instantly, Champion slammed on her brakes, pressing her passengers forcefully against their seatbelts. Unrestrained, however, Buddy was abruptly catapulted out of his basket, flying over the guard rail and into the marsh.

"Buddy!" Champion screamed, frantically unhooking her seatbelt.

The next sound heard was a loud splash as Ryan dove over the barrier and grabbed the floundering 30-pound dog. Movement in the water just feet away revealed the snout of a swiftly approaching alligator. With Buddy tightly gripped in his hands, Ryan leaped back over the barrier, dripping black mud that also splattered the trembling little dog.

"My God!" Champion exclaimed, tearfully cradling

her prized pet before collapsing onto her cart seat. "I almost lost my baby. You were magnificent," she said to Ryan.

"Great work, Kevin" Del congratulated. "You're stealing my thunder."

"Just routine SEAL morning limbering-up exercises," Ryan replied, wiping muddy water from his eyes.

"Your old organization would be proud of you," Dutton said with admiration.

"Your current one as well," Chen added, "and it looks like you've adopted some of Del's fabulous luck."

"Wow. That was so cool," one of the youthful bicyclists addressed Ryan. "That alligator was only a foot away. It must have been ten feet long!"

"You're a hero!" the other youth proclaimed. "What do you have to say?"

Ryan grinned at the teen-aged girl. "Stay out of the marshes."

With adrenalin and heartbeats abating, the group regained their seats in the cart. "I need to give Buddy a bath when we get back," Champion declared.

"Think I'll wash off with a swim in the ocean," Ryan said.

Del and Anna hugged each other.

Dutton sighed, then smiled. "I always expected such machinations from Dickerson. Now I have to keep an eye on Ryan."

"What happened to my quiet little island?" Champion wondered.

JIM HEALY

*Captain Charlie's Station* - Bald Head Island Rescue Station
Mixed Water Media Painting by Sarah Hasty Williams

## Chapter Twenty

Olga Servadova's famed goulash was being enthusiastically devoured in Dutton's rental cottage at a large picnic table on an expansive screened porch.

"You have outdone yourself, Olga. It's better than ever," Dutton complimented.

"Exquisite," Peggy Champion praised as she ate with one hand and cradled Buddy in the other.

The sturdy cook beamed brightly. "My honor," she said, "and a special treat for Mr. Ryan, who I heard saved that little sabatchka from an alligator."

"He didn't hesitate to act," Chen said with admiration. "We have a room full of heroes."

"You have a stable of handsome FBI agents," Nadia Rostov said, reminding the group of her boyfriend, Curt Oswald, the agent who befriended her in the FBI's recent SPYTRAP special.

Tanya Tamarof flashed a knowing smile. "I noticed the same thing," she said referring to Joe Moretti the agent she met in the same investigation who became a regular patron of her Tae Kwon Do studio.

"Wait till you hear about some of Andy Dutton's exploits," Del said. "He's a living legend."

"Okay," Dutton interrupted, "enough of this self-adulation. We have current business to address. I contacted Chuck Phillips, the retired Customs official we met, and he's calling some of his old associates to get a handle on what they know about local drug smuggling. I expect to hear from him soon."

Ryan put his spoon down, and sighed. "I don't want

to interfere with the enjoyment of your wonderful dish," he said to the cook, before turning to his fellow agents. "Just before lunch I received a call from Sheriff Lawson in Carolina Beach. He gave me the results of his inquiries around Rufus and Beau's boat dock."

"And?" Dutton asked.

"He finally interviewed a boater on their adjacent dock," Ryan related. "The guy, Rudy Dillon, was out of town until yesterday. Dillon said he recalled some unusual activity around the *Lucky Lady* the night Del disappeared. He said he was asleep in his cabin sometime after midnight. No lights were on, and his boat probably looked unoccupied. Anyway, something awakened him and he looked out a porthole and saw two figures hauling a large sack onto the *Lucky Lady*. Dillon said he wasn't sure it was Chamberlin and Reynolds, because of the darkness, but assumed it was them. He said he then heard their motors start and saw the boat move away from the dock. Dillon went back to sleep, but woke up again a couple of hours later. He didn't see anyone on the *Lucky Lady* when he went ashore the next morning. Dillon added that it was an unusual time to go out to sea and return so quickly."

"It's beginning to fit together," Del said. "I believe it's time to revisit Carolina Beach. I'm sure I can identify the guys I encountered in Captain Bill's back room."

"If we can find them," Ryan observed. "The sheriff said they haven't been seen around town lately."

"Maybe Captain Bill can shed some light," Del said with a determined expression.

"I'm anxious to talk with that lying bastard again," Ryan said, massaging his knuckles.

"It's about an hour away to Southport. Let's inform the ladies at Peggy's cottage and head for the ferry."

"What about me?" Anna Chen asked. "I was just reunited with Del."

"Stay with Jenny, Leigh, and me," Champion comforted. "Let the men handle their business while we gals relax. We'll bail them out when they get into trouble again."

"We won't be gone long," Del assured his fiancée.

"Okay," Chen said reluctantly. "Only no more bumps on your head. You're just beginning to make sense."

"Don't worry," Del said, bending to kiss her, and stumbling over a waste basket and almost falling.

Chen closed her eyes and mentally prayed an ancient Chinese proverb.

## SOUTHPORT

"Where the hell have you been?" Ramon Montez angrily demanded in his cell communication.

"Kind of lying low while waiting for the shipment," Rufus Reynolds replied in an apologetic voice.

"Why?" Montez pressed. "'What are you worried about? Are you two in some kind of trouble?"

"Well, we're being harassed by some goons."

"Goons? Like what?"

"Ah," Reynolds responded. "The local sheriff and some asshole FBI agents."

"The sheriff and the FBI! What in hell did you guys do?"

"We didn't want to bother you with such small details." Reynolds nervously replied.

"Madre Christo!" Montez screamed. "What are the small details?"

Reynolds stumbled ahead. "It all happened when Beau clubbed the guy who busted into the counting room."

"You was there too," a voice could be heard yelling from the background.

"So what happened next?" Montez asked in a worried tone.

"Well," Reynolds continued, "the guy looked dead, so we stuffed him in a sack and took him out on our boat and dumped him overboard."

"Hmm," Montez remarked in a calmer voice, "that should have solved your unfortunate problem. Not too smart, but effective. We occasionally need severe action to safeguard our valuable business. So what's the problem?"

"Thanks for your understanding, Ramon. You're a good man. To get to the point, the guy Beau slugged was an FBI agent."

"Jesus!" Montez cursed.

"There's more," Reynolds quickly followed. "He's still alive. He washed up on Bald Head Island."

"Deo magnifico!" Montez moaned. "You have put us all in peril."

"That's why we're lying low," Reynolds informed. "The police and FBI are asking all kinds of questions around Carolina Beach."

"Do you have any idea what the Commander will do if he finds this out?" Montez asked.

"I know he don't like mistakes," Reynolds admitted.

"Right!" Beau Chamberlin could be heard agreeing in the background.

"At least you had the brains to get lost," Montez said in a more controlled voice. "Where are you?"

"In a dump motel in Leland, on the edge of Wilmington. Beau thinks it's got bedbugs. He's been scratching like hell."

Serves you right, Montez thought before replying. "Stay put. The shipment is due any day, and you are essential in unloading. I'll be back in touch."

"You handled that good," Beau Chamberlin complimented his cousin, scratching his crotch. "We got nothing to worry about."

Reynolds shook his head and picked up his rum bottle. "I need some more coke. There's a 7 Eleven down the street."

"Good," Chamberlin replied. "I can use a giant Slurpee and some itch powder."

## Chapter Twenty-one

SOUTHPORT

Less than two miles from Ramon's Fresh Catch market, Dutton, Ryan and Del debarked from the ferry boat *Ranger* after a twenty-five minute voyage from Bald Head Island.

"We go through Wilmington on the way to Carolina Beach," Dutton noted. "Let's drop in at their Resident Agency and inform them what we're doing in their territory."

"Good idea." Ryan agreed. "I'm sure Brad Evans apprised the senior R.A. of that, but we might learn what they have on the local drug smuggling situation."

\* \* \*

Inside Ramon's Fresh Catch store, the proprietor was surveying the near-empty shelves of the concealed freezer located at the rear of his building. They should soon be jammed with precious bags worth a fortune, was his thought, if those two clowns don't screw up the entire operation. Why didn't I replace them earlier? he ruminated. Should I inform the Commander, he asked himself. Extinguishing the lights and engaging the sturdy door lock, Montez decided to defer notifying his superior. Why test the Commander's wrath, he reasoned. That could prove fatal.

LELAND, NC

"I could use a cup of coffee," Ryan announced from

the driver's seat of their SUV stopped at a traffic light in the small community bordering Wilmington.

"There's a 7-Eleven on the far corner," Dutton pointed out. "Good enough?"

"Fine with me" Ryan replied.

"I'll stay in the car," Del said from a back seat where he had been dozing. Re-closing his eyes, Del was happily reflecting on the passionate reunion with his fiancée the previous evening, when the loud slamming of a car door jarred him from his semi-slumber. Studying his surroundings, Del's attention was attracted to a pair of men emerging from the store. Suddenly wide awake, he shouted aloud "It's them!" and began unlatching his seat belt, while scanning the parking area for his two companions. By the time he exited the SUV, he caught a glimpse of the two men climbing into a silver-colored van and driving off, its license plate out of his line of sight.

Dutton and Ryan emerged from the store to find Del staring with frustration into the distance. "It was them!" Del yelled, pointing at the disappearing vehicle. "The guys from Captain Bill's. Let's go after them!"

All eyed the heavy traffic clogging the intersection. "You sure it was them?" Dutton asked as they hurried into their vehicle.

"90 % sure" Del asserted.

"Damn," Ryan exclaimed, seeing a large Budweiser delivery truck blocking their exit from their parking space. By the time its driver moved his long trailer, several intersection light changes had occurred, rendering pursuit futile. Dutton patted Del's shoulder. "Your fabled luck must have taken a break," he consoled. "But at least we know they're somewhere around. I'll ask the R.A. to issue a BOLO for any licenses issued in their names. We'll find them. It'll just take a little longer."

Ryan added his condolences. "I've mentioned before a SEAL slogan, *'The only easy day was yesterday.'*"

## WILMINGTON, NC

Special Agent Brad Evans welcomed them to the Wilmington Resident Agency, a sub-office of the FBI's Charlotte Division. "We have ten agents, plus a like number of support personnel," Evans informed, "but we are also partnered with a number of law enforcement task forces in the area, including one of particular interest to the Senior R.A. He's anxious to discuss it with you. Will Hudgins is his name, a good guy, whose ears perked up when I mentioned the drug circumstances at Carolina Beach. He's waiting in his office."

Hudgins and Dutton immediately recognized each other from past investigative encounters over the years. Pleasantries were shared and welcomes extended to Ryan and Del. Hudgins listened with growing interest to a summary of Del's experiences in Carolina Beach and Bald Head Island before slapping his hand on his well-polished walnut desk. "This could be the break we've been looking for," he declared. "We're all well aware of the current drug plague affecting the East Coast, and the relentless efforts of drug smugglers to supply the demands of their users. To combat that scourge there's a major Task Force, of which we are a prominent member. It's comprised of DEA, Customs, Coast Guard, Navy, North Carolina State Bureau of Investigation, CIA and FBI. Leadership varies depending on the particular problem, but currently DEA is the lead agency in this situation, with our immediate support. And, it just so happens that a briefing on the present state of an ongoing smuggling operation is scheduled for this afternoon. You might find it especially relevant based on what you've discovered. Are you able to attend?"

"No question," Dutton answered for the trio. "That's why we're here."

\* \* \*

The group meeting was held in a large DEA conference room in its Wilmington office. Drug Enforcement Agency Special Agent in Charge Dwight Hawkins, a tall, trim African-American, presided. At least twenty additional representatives of various agencies were present, and Hawkins mentioned each by name. "We've been tracking the latest entry attempt to penetrate the East Coast," he began. "It's a major endeavor that will test our best defenses. Everyone's seen their growing sophistication involving planes, drones, helos, balloons, parachutes, tunnels-- you name it. The Coast Guard has been particularly effective in seizing cargoes at sea," Hawkins said, in a nod in the direction of a Coast Guard officer. "Interdiction of their semi-submersible subs worked for a while, but as soon as we plug one hole, they open another. The latest threat is a load of cocaine headed our way from Colombia, a cargo with an estimated street value of almost five-hundred million dollars. It's coming via one of their most ambitious methods, a state-of-the art mini sub, designed and built in Russia, then assembled in Colombia."

Hawkins paused and scanned his audience. "We

all know the brutality of our adversaries. Until recently we were receiving good intel on the progress of this operation. Then the flow of information suddenly stopped. We just learned that our informant was murdered, and not too gently. He was hacked to pieces and thrown to the alligators. Life is cheap there," he remarked grimly.

"So, to summarize, we know a load of cocaine worth almost a half-billion dollars is headed to the East Coast via a new, sophisticated submarine, reportedly due to arrive somewhere on our coast within a few days. All agencies are requested to employ every available resource to address this threat, and immediately share any relevant information. DEA has been designated lead in this investigation, with primary support of FBI, which has an agent who was recently attacked and left for dead close to here by suspected members of this plot." Hawkins nodded at Del. "We're happy you survived, and understand you're a good swimmer with fantastic luck. We can certainly use some of that here. Finally, to coordinate what will probably be a fast moving operation, it has been assigned the FBI code name SEACATCH."

As the conference concluded with various task force members exchanging information, the Customs representative approached Dutton. "Wayne Jackson," the man said, introducing himself and producing a business card identifying himself as a Customs Special Agent. "Chuck Phillips called me and mentioned your contact. He's an old friend, and had an outstanding record with our service. Let me know what we can do to help."

Dutton thanked Jackson, promising to be in touch. "Looks like we're involved in a bigger deal than we imagined," Dutton said to Del and Ryan. "I should have expected that anything Del touches would be special," he added with a grin. "How about moving on now to Carolina Beach? I'm anxious to meet Captain Bill."

## Chapter Twenty-two

CAROLINA BEACH

They met in the oceanfront lounge of the Hampton Inn with Deputy Sheriff Lyle Lawson.

Dutton filled him in on what they had learned on the scope of the ongoing major smuggling operation.

Lawson smiled at Del. "Never imagined our initial contact would become this big, Del. Where do we go from here?"

"The reason for our meet," Dutton said, "is to determine what's the best approach. I'm thinking soft at first, with succeeding step-ups," he said, proceeding to enumerate his suggestions. Nods of agreement concluded the gathering, and they headed for Captain Bill's Sea Catch.

What a dump was Dutton's thought as he entered alone through a battered door that must have bruised the arms and heads of countless drunken patrons. Proceeding into the dimly lit atmosphere that reeked of beer, he took a seat at the lightly patronized bar and asked the barmaid to see Captain Bill. The thin bleached blonde with uneven stained teeth, wearing a pink tank top and brief denim shorts paused. "Don't ya wanta drink first? Folks usually do before they see him."

"Guess that would be in order," Dutton replied. "Fill a pitcher with your house draft and bring it to a table with four glasses."

"Four glasses?"

"Yes, Four glasses. I assume you have that many.

I'm expecting company."

"Sure, mister. Can I tell Captain Bill your name?"

"Dutton. FBI," he announced, watching the barmaid scurry quickly away.

Dutton was seated at a rickety table near the rear of the room minutes later with a sweaty pitcher of draft beer before him, and a half-empty glass in his hand when the proprietor arrived.

Scruffy appearance, two-day beard, bulbous, vein-streaked nose, soiled jeans and scratched sandals were Dutton's instant assessment.

"Scat Killer!" Captain Bill shouted at a large mangy cat that scurried off a chair. "Get to work! Keeps down the rat population," he muttered, "except when they are too big," he added with a glare at his visitor.

"FBI, eh?" Captain Bill Andrews finally greeted, studying Dutton's proffered credentials.

"And, Special Agent in Charge! They're moving in the big guns. What do you want?"

"Answers, Mr. Andrews. That's the name we'd like to use. We are seeking your cooperation as a good citizen. The last time my associates visited, they were requesting help in finding a colleague last seen in your establishment."

"Yeah and I told them no one recalled seeing him here."

"Including the waitress, who was subsequently found murdered."

"Far from here.'" Andrews quickly snapped. "That was too bad. She used to bring in the business--big tits, cute ass."

"Is that what she meant to you? I hear she had children and was a hard worker."

"Yeah, she was popular. The bar sent flowers to her funeral. Half the men in town attended," he giggled.

Dutton shook his head. "Including Beau Chamberlin and Rufus Reynolds?"

"Haven't seen them lately. They never spent much time here anyway."

"That's not what we've heard."

"Hope you don't believe everything you hear, Inspector."

"Inspector was a long time ago, Andrews. We're not overwhelmed with titles. When it comes to doing the job, we're all equal, which is why we were so concerned over losing our friend in your bar."

Andrews reared back. "I think you're trying to intimidate me. If you don't have anything more, I think you're wasting my time, which I believe means wasting taxpayer money."

"We always want hard-working taxpayers like you to get their money's worth," Dutton said, reaching into his trouser pocket to click his iPhone. He then began filling a glass from the imposing beer pitcher. A minute later Kevin Ryan strode through the door, brushing against an errant chair that toppled to the floor.

Andrews looked up with alarm. "That's the guy who busted up my furniture the last time!"

Ryan smiled as he straddled a chair and enthusiastically attacked the waiting glass of beer. "We're just here to see if your memory has improved after a period of reflection. It sometimes happens. Has anything occurred to you?"

Perspiration formed on Andrew's forehead as he

looked nervously toward the door while Ryan filled another glass. "Something to jar your memory?" Ryan asked, nodding towards Del walking their way.

"Remember me now?" Del addressed Andrews. "This is the last place I remember having a beer."

Andrews slouched back in a defensive position. "Never saw you before in my life," he declared emphatically.

"How about Beau and Rufus?"

"They used to drop in occasionally."

"How about your back room?"

"Every store has a back room. A law against that?"

"How about rest rooms?"

"Sure. Law requires them."

"May I see yours? They have unusual names -- Buoys and Gulls, I recall."

Andrews looked increasingly nervous, studying the beer pitcher. "Guess, since you bought something, I can't deny you the use of the facilities."

"Thanks for your increasing cooperation,'" Del said, leading the group along a dim hall to the restroom area that featured three doors, a coin telephone, a condom machine, and a fourth, distant door with an emergency exit sign. "I remember these," Del stated, pointing at the hand-carved wooden cutouts, Buoys painted red for men, Gulls colored blue/gray for women. The door next to Buoys displayed a gold-painted plastic PRIVATE sign, and two sturdy locks.

"What's in there?" Dutton asked.

"Don't they teach you Inspectors to read?" Andrews said defiantly. "It says Private."

"We're asking respectfully to allow us to look inside," Dutton said.

"Respectfully," Andrews responded, "Fuck you. Get a warrant!"

Dutton nodded. "Guess that terminates our cordial cooperation," he said, waving to Sheriff Lyle Lawson who had arrived at the end of the visiting group, gripping the fourth beer glass.

"Have something for you," Lawson told Andrews, handing him a sheaf of papers.

"Notices from the state Alcohol Beverage Control, and the Health Department, shutting you down within thirty days. Might get you through Memorial Day, but you'll be dark for the Fourth."

"Sons of bitches," Andrews swore, grabbing the papers.

Dutton handed Andrews his business card. "Give me a call if you somehow learn the whereabouts of Beau and Rufus. It could have been so much easier with a little cooperation, Captain Bill. There's a twenty on the table for the beer. No gratuities accepted. Hope you have a flourishing business with your new law enforcement customers."

"Screw you!" were Andrews's parting words.

\* \* \*

"I believe we left a message," Sheriff Lawson said as the group lingered outside Captain Bill's Sea Shack. An approaching truck with four weathered fisherman slowed near an open parking space, then moved on when it's occupants spotted the marked police cruiser. Lawson grinned. "You might be getting a call soon," he said to Dutton. "A little heat can gradually boil a tough egg. By the way, the DNA is not back yet on Rufus, and there's been no sight of either of them lately. We're making spot checks on their boat, but haven't seen any movement. We're gearing up for the Memorial Day celebration. The area will be jammed with visitors. There will be lots of boats off shore, easy for one to get lost in the crowd. We'll stay alert."

"Thanks again for the help," Dutton told the sheriff. "I anticipate further collaboration with you soon. Now, we need to hurry to catch the last ferry to Bald Head Island."

Del headed for the car. "Believe me, it has to be healthier to be there than in Captain Bill's. Let's move it."

## Chapter Twenty-three

### SOUTHPORT

The twin-hulled ferry *Ranger* had signaled its final departure when the weary trio raced up the gangway. "We made it," Dutton said, collapsing into a cabin seat as the diesel engines propelled the craft from the dock.

"Lots to digest," Ryan commented. "Looks like we're on the brink of major action. We need to rest up and prepare," he said, leaning back and visualizing a career of hair-raising operations as a Navy SEAL. His eyes were soon closed.

Del nodded towards Ryan, "Mr. Cool. I think he's got the secret. I hear the ladies have scheduled a morning on the beach, followed by a seafood brunch. Any objections?" He looked at his partners. The drone of the boat's engines had Dutton fighting to remain awake. Ryan was already in recuperative slumber. Unanimous verdict, Del told himself, joining the party until the *Ranger* bumped the Bald Head Island Harbor Dock twenty-five minutes later.

### BALD HEAD ISLAND

Like a nighttime angel of mercy, Peggy Champion met the tired travelers in her six-passenger electric cart. She was accompanied by Anna Chen and Rambo. Buddy rested in his favorite basket next to Peggy. "Your welcoming committee," she announced in her typical upbeat spirit. "Didn't want you to end up in a ditch on our dark trails. You've seen the little ground-level, down-cast lights installed to safeguard our multitude of nesting turtles. Very little illumination. Can't say we aren't environmentally pure."

"Another wonderful discovery," Anna said, hugging her fiancé. "It's a relief having you back, safe, sound, and dry."

"Amen," Del agreed. "We confirmed the site of my last visit to Captain Bill's, and learned that my two possible assailants have disappeared. But, we got a glimpse of two guys I'm sure was them up near Wilmington. They have to be close."

Dutton interjected. "We also learned about a high-powered smuggling activity about to explode. They will be subjects of heavy discussion once we get some rest."

Ryan yawned. "Fresh batteries produce brighter lights."

"Another SEAL saying?" Del asked.

"No, Mother Ryan's sage advice her son learned at an early age."

"Smart mom," Champion said, reminding them of the planned morning beach party. "Leigh, Jenny, and Lydia, under Olga's energetic supervision, are creating a feast to follow sun and fun. The men can do their plotting while the women do all the work as usual, right Rambo?"

"Arf!" was the response as the cart carefully weaved through the island's dark forest canopy.

Bright and sunny late April weather distinguished the morning when the cheery group assembled on the beach across the road and crested dunes from Dutton's rental cottage. Champion's cart that had delivered her guests was parked on the access road to the water. Beach towels, colorful umbrellas, chairs, and coolers signaled a party. Other beach goers were scattered in the distance. Soft drinks, water, and Heinekens seemed to be the beverages of choice, interspersed with semi-frozen daiquiris.

"Hard to get better than this," Ryan declared, stretching out on a towel embossed with dolphins, not oblivious to the new string bikinis barely clothing Nadia Rostov and Tanya Tamarof. Nadia's was iridescent pink, minimal at best, proclaiming her provocative body. Tanya's black thong contrasted with her curly blonde hair, again leaving little to the imagination. The other women were garbed considerably more modestly. The men wore mundane swim shorts and T-shirts. Ryan's displayed a SEAL trident, Del's his Yale black Y, Dutton's a gold FBI agent's badge.

"No problem identifying you gents if you go too far," Champion commented with a laugh. "Watch for the undertow and rip currents," she cautioned.

"I invited Chuck Phillips to join us," Dutton informed. "He's the guy who came up with the information about the incoming drug load, which looks like a big deal."

"Right," Ryan agreed. "Everyone's on high alert, particularly with a fancy new sub involved. Someone with big bucks is pulling some big strings behind it all."

\* \* \*

Barely two miles away, former Navy Commander Randy King was welcoming his special guest to his secluded cottage. "I hope you didn't mind the ride over from the mainland on the back of Ramon's Sea-Doo."

"No, it was exhilarating, and the water spray as refreshing as the Black Sea," Colonel Serge Petrov remarked as he admired King's impressive surroundings. "You live well, Commander. I can see our collaboration has been beneficial."

"And yours too, Serge--even more so with the latest delivery due within hours. Now, how about a toast to this brilliant operation? I'm having Johnny Walker Blue. You?"

The husky Russian grinned. "What else but vodka?"

"Just as I anticipated," King declared, reaching for a fifth of Beluga Gold Line. He poured a half glass. "Salute!" he toasted.

"Zdarovye " (cheers), the Russian replied.

## Chapter Twenty-four

While the beachgoers raked in the penetrating sun rays under layers of sun block and the semi-shelter of beach umbrellas, Rambo and Buddy engaged in periodic tugs of war with a deflated beach ball. The elusive sandpipers and sea gulls frisking in the surf had finally convinced them of the futility of chasing them. An Island public safety officer on a four-wheel beach vehicle had just left the group with a friendly greeting, and caution about undertows and rip tides when Nadia Rostov and Tanya Tamarof announced it was time to cool off in the water. Minutes later they plunged into the breaking waves and were frolicking in the undulating sea.

"Don't go out too far," Champion warned as some of the others ventured into the water.

Leigh Daly, a former collegiate swimmer, returned closer to shore after an energetic venture into deeper water to announce a strong current running. Nadia and Tanya remained in the deeper water, swimming back and forth, playing tag with each other.

Dutton, Del, and Ryan interrupted their business session and were entering the water when Rambo began barking loudly in the direction of Nadia and Tanya who were now waving frantically for help. Closer inspection revealed that they had both removed their minimal tops that were now waving wildly.

"They're caught in a rip current," Ryan yelled. "They can't get back fighting it. They have to swim with it until there's a break. Let's go," he shouted, diving into the surf, immediately followed by Del who called to Dutton, "two's enough. We need someone on shore to do the report."

Within minutes the rescuers were close to the women who remained afloat in a relatively calm trough. "Keep calm and don't panic," the former SEAL told the women. "You're in good hands."

"Like Allstate?" Tanya quipped as Ryan reached her side.

"Thanks for coming," Nadia calmly told Del.

"I see you're in your birthday suit again, Nadia. Naughty girl."

"Naughty but nice? We always seem to end up like this. Fate?"

"Okay, listen up," Ryan interrupted, "here's what we do. We use the cross-chest carry and move parallel to the beach until there's a break in the current, then we swim through to shallow water. Ladies float on their backs, fluttering hands and feet. Got it?"

Nods of assent were vigorous.

"I have Tanya. Del, you take Nadia and let's get going. It's cold out here."

Ryan led the way, Del and Nadia following, his arm grasped her across her chest. With each side stroke, he glimpsed her ample breasts peeking through, hardened nipples seemingly winking at him.

After several strenuous minutes, Ryan reached a break where the tide shifted, and he headed to shore with Tanya. Del and Nadia quickly followed, everyone rejoicing in a sense of deliverance.

"Thank you, my hero," Tanya told Ryan. "You were magnificent," she said, affixing a wet kiss. "I'm surprised that Nadia didn't react better, she was a Russian Olympic swimmer, you know."

Ryan's expression indicated understanding.

"I owe you my life again," Nadia gasped to Del as they neared shore. "You're a strong swimmer."

Del emitted a knowing smile. "As are you, Nadia. I've read your background file, you know."

Nadia smiled.

The shoreline welcoming assemblage shouted relief and congratulations to the survivors, rushing to cover the shivering women.

Nadia fell into a beach chair. "Del saved me again."

Anna Chen hugged her fiancé and smiled at Nadia. "He does always seem to be where you need him, doesn't he?"

\* \* \*

The seafood cookout was a joyful celebration, the warming sun restoring the swimmers to normal body temperatures. Peggy Champion produced windbreakers from her cart that now modestly encased Nadia and Tanya. Restorative beverages were being enthusiastically consumed, everyone rejoicing in the rescue.

Chuck Phillips arrived with another man who he introduced as his twin brother, John. "He joined us at the Inn last night, and I took the liberty of bringing him along."

"The more the merrier," Dutton said in a welcoming tone as he studied the brother. "A spitting image," he declared. "Do you often get mistaken for each other?"

"All the time," Phillips chuckled, "except when the

dinner check arrives and he acts like we're strangers. Only difference is, he was too busy practicing as a veterinarian to get married, and spends his spare time singing at country music events."

Dutton proceeded to introduce the twins to his group, and soon the gregarious veterinarian was engaged in a spirited conversation with Leigh Daly, who enthused about her interest in fostering new-born kittens rescued from pet shelters.

Police Chief Martin dropped by to hear details of the ordeal, and congratulate Ryan and Del for their efforts. "That's usually our job," he said. "It doesn't always end up on a happy note. Good work." He also spent extra time talking with Jenny Miller, leaving her with a warm smile on her face.

"He's a recent widower," Peggy Champion mentioned to Jenny as he drove away. "He seemed quite attentive to you. I understand he's an artist. Isn't that your avocation? He's rather attractive, to boot."

Jenny Miller blushed. "I'm still grieving, you know."

Champion nodded understanding. "Just something to keep in mind, Jenny. You're an attractive woman, so don't be surprised that men will be interested in knowing you better. Only an observation from your loving cousin. Look at Leigh. She seems to be getting along famously with the former Customs agent's brother. Can't hear what they're talking about, but Andy Dutton said he's quite a singer. Maybe they're discussing making music together. She plays a mean piano, as we know."

Miller reached out to pat her cousin's arm. "You're

not only a great hostess, Peggy, but a blooming matchmaker as well. Thanks for your advice."

Their private discourse was interrupted by Olga Servadova's booming announcement: "Eat up everyone! Much good stuff. Made in America!"

Contented looks prevailed as the brunch disappeared and the relaxed beach ambiance prompted yawns and drowsy eyes with the backdrop of gentle waves lapping at the shore. "I think I'm going to enjoy retirement," Dutton was commenting to Kevin Ryan when the musical tones of *God Bless America* sounded on his iPhone. Dutton listened attentively to the brief message, asked a couple of questions that were quickly answered, and hung up.

"Time to saddle up," he told his investigative colleagues. "It's going down around Carolina Beach, and we need to head that way. That was Hawkins, the DEA SAC. They were just informed of a NSA satellite intercept that the sub and its drug payload is due to arrive near Carolina Beach tomorrow night. That's Memorial Day, of course. Should be lots of fireworks, in more ways than one. So, pack up guys. We need to catch the next ferry out."

"There's a big Memorial Day celebration here tomorrow night," Peggy Champion reminded. "I hoped we could all celebrate together."

Dutton's wife, Lydia, smiled. "I've heard this song before." Leigh Daly added her thoughts, recalling her years as an FBI wife. "The men are off to battle again. We wait at home, hoping and praying."

## Chapter Twenty-five

CAROLINA BEACH

Sheriff Lyle Lawson met them at the Hampton Inn where he used his law enforcement clout to secure rooms in the otherwise packed hotel. "The town is jammed for the holiday, as you can see from the street traffic. It's the first big holiday weekend of the season and everyone's eager for sun and fun. A big fireworks display is scheduled off shore for tomorrow night."

"In the midst of the drug delivery," Ryan observed. "Well planned."

Lawson nodded. "And there will be a slew of boats floating around to observe the festivities."

"Including several of ours--DEA, Customs, Coast Guard, Navy, according to the DEA SAC," Dutton informed. "It could get very crowded."

"What about Beau and Rufus' *Lucky Lady*?" Del asked. "I have a score to settle with them."

"We've been spot checking," Lawson responded with a sheepish look, "but they moved it out the night before last, before my man got there."

"Damn," Del said.

"But we found it in a small marina a little north of Wilmington," Lawson added in a more upbeat tone.

"That's encouraging." Del said.

Lawson continued. "It had a section of canvas draped across its stern, covering its name."

"So we know where it is?"

"Did," Lawson went on with a frown. "It moved out sometime last night, current location unknown."

"Double damn," Del allowed.

"Yeah," Lawson agreed, "but on a more positive note, we finally received the DNA results on the skin found under the fingernails--a definite match to the murdered waitress, Wanda Somerset. We should be able to put Reynolds away for a long time."

"Bastard," Del cursed. "She didn't deserve to die like that."

"Justice will prevail," Dutton consoled. "Get some sleep. There's an eight a.m. conference of the Strike Force in Wilmington tomorrow. It will be a long day."

"Ready to rock and roll," Ryan said. "About time for some action."

Del nodded agreement. "Lots of unfinished business to conclude, and I don't plan to be floating to Bald Head Island this time."

Ryan had the last word, reaching into a Walmart bag to extract a set of water wings which he presented to Del. "Just in case," he joked.

Dutton looked at his unpredictable young colleague, then back at Ryan. "Kevin, we've both seen what can happen when he's involved. Keep your jock tight."

Del looked bewildered. "What are you guys talking about? I'm just a little black sheep who has gone astray. Baa, baa, baa."

## WILMINGTON, NC

It was an energized group of law enforcement personnel assembled in the DEA conference room. DEA Special Agent in Charge Dwight Hawkins presided, informing at the outset that a NSA satellite recently intercepted a cryptic message from the incoming submarine, indicating an off-loading rendezvous that evening. "Additionally interesting," he proceeded, "are presumably related messages to a building on Bald Head Island, and, if you can believe it, to an office in the Pentagon!"

"Holy moly!" Del whispered to his companions. "The Pentagon! That's a new wrinkle."

Hawkins proceeded to enumerate the personnel and equipment assembled to cover the drug transfer. "We're relying heavily on Coast Guard, Navy, and Customs assets, along with some of ours," he added. "FBI personnel will be with me on the command boat, and all units will communicate on a dedicated radio channel. Any questions?"

A flood of relevant questions followed, with the session concluding an hour later, the participants dispersing to prepare for the coming action. As the FBI trio headed out, they encountered former Customs agent Chuck Phillips, who was talking with the ranking Customs official who he introduced as Barney Swift.

"Barney invited me to join the fun," Phillips advised with a bright smile. "He said that my Navy Reserve commission, and retired Customs status qualified me to be deputized for this mission, so here I am."

"Sounds logical to me," Dutton agreed.

"We'll be on a forty-foot Customs Sea Hunter," Swift added. "Lots of power and armament."

Dutton looked worried. "I understand there will be a lot of pleasure boats milling around offshore for the fireworks display. I hope we don't end up in traffic"

"Let's hope Murphy's Law will take a night off," said Ryan. "Sure don't need that curse tonight."

## WRIGHTSVILLE BEACH, NC

"Don't know why Ramon had to bring his damn Sea-Doo," Beau Chamberlin was complaining to Rufus Reynolds. "Almost gave me a hernia hauling it aboard, and it cuts into the space we have for the goods."

"Yeah, it's in the way, but I'm not about to argue with him. He said the boss ordered him to be with us. Ramon has a hot temper, you know."

"Spics usually have them, Rufus, along with their switchblades," he said, gesturing in the direction of Montez who was securing his watercraft to the *LUCKY LADY*.

"At least he left his damned trailer behind. We sure didn't have room for that."

"Yeah, Beau, it's lowering our storage space. We need it all for the good stuff."

"And, he's got a gun," Chamberlin said. "Hope there's no shooting. I hate violence."

"Like when you damned near killed that FBI agent with a beer bottle?"

"That was self-defense, Rufus. He was invading our privacy. And you should talk. How about you taking out Wanda? You're in big trouble."

"You too, Beau. You was a cessory."

"I'll be glad when this delivery is over, Rufus, and we can get our payoff and head for the hills."

"Good with me. Now let's get our tanks filled and be ready to head south. The sub's due around nine."

## CAROLINA BEACH

Deputy Sheriff Lyle Lawson, and agents of the North Carolina Bureau of Investigation came aboard Hawkins' boat and found the FBI trio. Lawson tapped a uniform pocket. "Murder warrant for Rufus Reynolds, to add to his forthcoming additional charges. Should be a memorable day for him."

FBI agent Brad Evans from the Wilmington Resident Agency also appeared. "Finally going down," he said, looking around at the assortment of law enforcement personnel. "Biggest joint task force I've ever seen."

"Everyone's got an interest in the case," Dutton acknowledged. "I just hope we don't get in each other's way. I've learned from experience that the more involved an operation is, the more things can go wrong. I prefer them simple and tight."

"Amen." Ryan said. "Too many cooks . . ."

"All we need is a little luck," Del interjected. "We're on the side of the angels."

"The legendary Dickerson luck would certainly help," Dutton said hopefully, pointing at a line of private pleasure boats beginning to assume positions about three miles offshore.

"The fireworks barge will operate in that area," Lawson informed. "The boaters like to be in the center of the action. This should be a Memorial Day to top all others. Talk about fireworks!"

## Chapter Twenty-six

NORTH CAROLINA SHORE

The high-powered armada of law enforcement watercraft remained concealed a strategic distance from the Carolina Beach oceanfront, striving to avoid attracting attention. Remote marinas and covered boat yards substantially masked their visibility. Coast Guard and Customs helicopters were strategically positioned at nearby heliports, ready for immediate response. Skilled land, sea, and air personnel waited anxiously for the starting signal.

"It's the waiting that wears you down," Dutton lamented to Del, pointing to Kevin Ryan who was dozing in a deck chair. "Except for ex-SEALS, it appears."

"Don't be fooled by appearances," Ryan interjected, lifting one eye. "Just resting my eyes and conserving energy. I'll be ready when the starting whistle blows."

AT SEA

"Our long voyage is almost over," Captain Carlos Alvarez told his sweaty crew members crammed between stacks of plastic-encased packets of cocaine. "Then our reward," he proclaimed with a glowing smile.

"I will be happy to receive my pay," Juan Esposito responded.

"And my family will celebrate with the food I can buy," added Herberto Menendez.

## WRIGHTSVILLE BEACH

"Almost dark," Rufus Reynolds announced to Chamberlin and Montez, as he started the engines of the *Lucky Lady*. "Time to head south. Hope the sub is where it's supposed to be."

"Don't worry," Montez assured. "The Commander plans things out to perfection. He knows what he's doing."

"Sure hope so," Chamberlin muttered to himself. "This whole deal is beginning to suck."

## CAROLINA BEACH

"Looks like a record crowd," the Manager of the Hampton Inn remarked to a reservation clerk. "Full house, overflowing beach, and clear skies for the fireworks which are about to begin," words no sooner uttered when booming sounds echoed from the ocean, followed by sparkling colors brightening the skies. Roars of approval rose from the beachside crowd. "Look at that Mabel!" one excited tourist exclaimed pointing at the glowing sky and sipping his frozen daiquiri.

As the fireworks barge ignited flares in rapid-fire sequence, the *Lucky Lady* hurried to a pre-set location where its crew watched with wonder as the narco sub slowly surfaced next to it. Immediately, plastic-encased kilos of high-quality Colombian cocaine were being passed from the sub to the *Lucky Lady*. Working at a feverish pace, the transfer was well underway below a sky-filled umbrella of exploding fireworks when a U.S. Coast Guard helicopter suddenly appeared overhead. Powerful searchlights illuminated the action below, accompanied by a firm loudspeaker message: "POLICE! This is the United States Coast Guard! You are under arrest! Stand by for boarding!" The message was repeated in Spanish as the roar of powerful law enforcement boats speeding to the scene reverberated across the water, accompanied by the wail of sirens and flashing blue and red lights.

That's when Murphy's Law intervened.

## Chapter Twenty-seven

"Holy shit," Beau Chamberlin exclaimed, slumping to the deck. Blinded by the brilliant searchlights, Rufus Reynolds and the sub crewmen did the same. Not so, did Ramon Montez and the sub captain. Both began firing at the helicopter, rounds from Montez's nine millimeter Sig Sauer connecting with the helicopter's searchlights, extinguishing two of them. Encouraged, Montez inserted another clip and resumed firing. From the deck of the sub, Captain Alvarez shouldered a M60 machine gun and began firing at the hovering aircraft.

Vacationing boater Wendell Avery, skipper of a 25-foot Bayliner idling some 300 feet from the action, stared with a near-panic expression. "Good Lord, I thought at first this was part of the celebration, but it's the real thing! Let's haul ass out of here," he declared to his guests, pushing forward on his throttle.

DEA Special Agent in Charge Dwight Hawkins, on the Task Force command boat, cursed to himself. "Fucking Murphy showed up," then issued an order to the converging law enforcement vessels: "Hold your fire. We have a pack of private watercraft all around the interception site."

As Hawkins' order was being honored, the sub captain continued to blast away at the helicopter, and bad turned to worse when one of his rounds punctured a hydraulic line feeding the jet turbine engine. Sparks flew, and a sudden loss of power forced the experienced pilot to auto rotate his float-equipped aircraft to a soft landing on the water. Law enforcement boats dodged the maze of private craft to rush to the rescue, with attention also remaining focused on the sub and the *Lucky Lady*.

"Just what I was afraid of," Dutton muttered, gripping a stanchion of the command boat racing through the melee.

Overhead, the grand finale of the fireworks brightened the skies, with rocket fragments drifting slowly to the ocean in the gentle winds.

Private pleasure craft were dispersing rapidly in all directions. "'What a show!" gushed a woman on Wendell Avery's boat that was headed north at flank speed.

"That wasn't a show, Gladys," Avery grimly replied, eyes glued to radar screen blips of other watercraft fleeing the scene. "We were lucky as hell to get out alive. Did you see the sub? We were in the middle of a big-time deal!"

Another private yacht was not so fortunate when it bolted across the bow of a racing Customs boat that struck it on the port bow, inflicting a sharp gash just above the water line. Emergency aid was afforded by the Customs crew, as both vessels rocked immobilized in the undulating sea.

"What a mess," Del declared as the command boat closed on their target. Tense fingers itched close to triggers of holstered weapons. "What else can go wrong?" he wondered at the same time bullets began to whiz by, one striking a gunwale uncomfortably close to Del's knee.

"They're shooting at us," a guardsman shouted. "Can we return fire?"

The DEA SAC hesitated only briefly before responding. "Not yet," he said decisively. "Too many private craft in the way, and too much danger of friendly cross fire. Let's get closer to the target."

Ryan looked grim but remained silent. Dutton shook his head in frustration before commenting, "He's probably right."

While sporadic bullets blazed by, their targets took some comfort from the protective vests they had donned before the raid.

"Our drone is delivering a good picture," Hawkins said, pointing to the monitor above the pilot-house control panel.

"'That's them for sure," Del affirmed as he stared at the two fishermen he had encountered just a few days before in Captain Bill's back room.

"Who's the third guy?" Ryan asked.

"Ramon Montez," Sheriff Lawson informed from his position in the cluster of engrossed officers. "He operates Ramon's Fresh Catch in Southport, and has been under suspicion for drug dealing."

"Well, this pretty well confirms that suspicion," Ryan commented wryly.

"Looks like four or five on the sub," Hawkins was saying when the screen went suddenly black. "'Damn," he moaned, "we lost our signal, or the drone may have been shot down."

"Par for the course tonight," Ryan agreed, peering out at the sky where occasional bullet flashes continued to flare.

"They're getting close," Rufus Reynolds yelled, "and I'm heading out of here. Hang on," he said, shouting to Captain Alvarez on the adjacent sub. "Follow me if you want. Ramon and I know a great hiding place."

"Lead on," Alvarez replied. "I don't have any more charts of the area."

The *Lucky Lady's* engines were soon propelling it at max speed in a southeasterly direction, moving roughly a mile or two ahead of the pursuing law enforcement craft.

Breaking free of the cluster of private boats, it was now a case of hot pursuit, with permission to return fire. A Navy helicopter that had been standing by, suddenly appeared in the sky, its powerful searchlights sweeping the ocean for the fleeing vessels.

"Where do you think they're heading?" Hawkins polled his colleagues.

"Unless they're aiming for an off-shore mother ship that we know nothing about, I'd guess they're heading for the Southport area," Dutton speculated. "They're familiar with the territory, and know places to hide."

Hawkins nodded understanding. "That's about twenty miles from here and they just changed course to due south."

"Can we intercept them before they reach that vicinity?" Dutton wondered.

"We're faster," Hawkins noted, "and we're currently only about two miles apart. Things are looking up. The Navy chopper found them, and have them lit up like a Christmas tree."

"It's about time for a break," Ryan spoke for the encouraged pursuers.

Del studied the monitors. "We have to be close to Bald Head Island. Feels like I've been here before."

# Chapter Twenty-eight

BALD HEAD ISLAND

The mood was festive at the crowded *Shoals Club,* celebrating patrons enthusing over the fireworks display that had just concluded on the nearby namesake shoals that projected jauntily into the Atlantic Ocean at the Point of Cape Fear.

Peggy Champion was hosting a large table of women that included Lydia Dutton, Anna Chen, Leigh Daly, Jenny Miller, Nadia Rostov, Tanya Tamarof, and Olga Servadova. "I wonder if the men are having as much fun," Champion questioned, raising her wine goblet in salute.

"They're supposed to be working." Lydia Dutton said. "I pray their anticipated raid was successful."

Anna Chen looked worried. "There is always so much danger, and Del seems to invariably be in the thick of it."

"But he always survives," Nadia Rostov observed with a knowing smile. "I'm betting on him."

"He good man," Olga Servadova proclaimed "He buy me new goulash pot, and he a lucky-ducky," she added with a bright smile. "Am I sounding like real American?"

"You're an All-American," Leigh Daly said, toasting the cook with her glass of chardonnay.

"I'm sure we'll hear from them as soon as it's over up there," Lydia Dutton predicted. "Too bad we couldn't witness the action."

## AT SEA

"They're running awfully close to shore," Hawkins remarked in the cockpit of the DEA pursuit boat. "My charts show a long stretch of shoals off Bald Head Island."

Aboard the *Lucky Lady* Ramon Montez scowled. "Can't you go any faster, Rufus? That copter is almost right above us."

"Going as fast as I can with the sub trailing behind," Reynold replied.

"Fuck the sub. Let's save ourselves."

"But what about all the stuff still on it?"

"Screw it, buddy. We have enough to make us fabulously rich if we can get away."

A demanding loudspeaker, accompanied with sirens and flashing blue and red lights from the hovering helicopter interrupted the debate: "This is the United States Navy commanding you to stop your craft immediately."

"What should we do?" Reynolds asked Montez.

"How far are we from the hiding place?" Montez asked.

Reynolds looked nervously upward. "Close. All we need to do is get around the point of Bald Head Island and we can get concealed, unload the shipment and hit the road."

"Let's give up," Beau Chamberlin implored. "Those choppers carry big guns, and you're getting us too close to shore. It's low tide. Don't forget the shoals."

"What?" Reynolds snorted. "Ya don't think I know how to pilot a boat? What a pussy!"

## SHOALS CLUB

"Look at the brilliant lights in the sky," Jenny Miller exclaimed, pointing from their patio table to the rapidly approaching aircraft's search lights.

"They're illuminating something on the water," Champion declared. "Wonder what it is?"

## AT SEA

"I tell ya, yur too close to shore," Beau Chamberlin was yelling at his cousin when the *Lucky Lady* came to an abrupt, shattering stop, throwing its three occupants to the deck, the power of the roaring outboard engines madly spinning the propellers in air as the boat's bow remained firmly imbedded in the sand bar.

"Told ya, asshole," Chamberlin shouted, coming to his feet and wiping a trickle of blood from his forehead.

"What the hell!" Montez screamed. "You ran us aground, you idiot!"

Rufus Reynolds had just stumbled upright when his blurry eyes widened to see the narco sub run up on the shoal some ten feet away. Bodies were visible scrambling through the open hatch. The Navy helicopter's searchlight fully illuminated the scene below, accompanied by the command: "You are under arrest!"

Chamberlin immediately raised his arms in surrender, but Ramon Montez scurried to his Sea-Doo, signaled to Reynolds for help, released its restraints, and shoved the craft over the side of the *Lucky Lady*. Hopping aboard, with Reynolds seated close behind him, Montez engaged the engine.

"What about me?" Chamberlin yelled at Reynolds. "Ya gonna leave me behind?"

"Don't be self-centered, Beau," Reynolds responded. "Think of someone else for a change."

"But we're cousins," Chamberlin implored.

"I was never quite sure of that," Reynolds shouted back. "Ya always looked a lot like crazy Uncle Louie. Good luck. It's every man for himself."

"But, Rufus . . ." Chamberlin was pleading when the Sea-Doo started moving.

"Adios Amigos," Ramon Montez shouted as he sped away into the night.

## Chapter Twenty-nine

DEA SAC Dwight Hawkins was breathing sighs of relief as reports flooded in informing of the sudden culmination of the chase.

"A SEAL team dropped to the vessels and took six men into custody, one from the *Lucky Lady* and five from the narco sub," he related. "Two men, Ramon Montez and the skipper of the fishing boat, Rufus Reynolds, fled on a Sea-Doo, and remain at large. And we are seeking the head of this operation that NSA intercepts have identified as a disgraced former Navy Commander, Randy King, who lives on Bald Head Island." Hawkins continued, "They recovered an estimated nine tons of cocaine, already neatly packaged for sale on U.S. streets. You have been informed of its projected total value of a half billion dollars. Quite a successful day, I'd say." As his audience nodded agreement, Hawkins went on. "The Navy has barges en route to remove the *Lucky Lady* and narco sub from the shoal. They're particularly enthusiastic about examining the sub and its latest upgrades."

"A happy ending is always a relief," Dutton congratulated Hawkins with a hearty hand shake. "Now we need to wrap up business with the Commander and the fugitives, and anyone else involved."

"And I have an arrest warrant to be delivered to one Rufus Reynolds," Sheriff Lyle Lawson added.

"Looks like we still have plenty of work to do," Dutton reminded. "I wonder how the ladies are doing?"

## SHOALS CLUB

"You sure know how to entertain your guests," Leigh Daly praised Peggy Champion as the patrons of the exclusive club watched with awe at the dramatic action unfolding before them. "It looks like the subjects the men were expecting near Carolina Beach," Daly speculated. "Wasn't it nice of them to bring the show to our neighborhood? Do you suppose any of them are on those boats with the flashing lights?"

Daly's question was answered when Lydia Dutton's iPhone chirped, delivering a brief message from her husband: "We're all OK, and are nearby, but have some mopping up to do. Keep the porch light on."

With Dutton's comforting message, the women refocused on the ongoing drama, especially on a helicopter whose floodlight was sweeping the ocean, supposedly searching for an elusive small object.

## ABOARD THE COMMAND BOAT

"Where do you think they're heading?" Hawkins questioned, studying his charts.

"Well, they initially headed East," Dutton noted, "and some of our boats are looking there. How fast can the Sea-Doo go?"

"Up to 60 miles per hour," Hawkins answered. "Faster than any of our boats."

"He might make a run around the Cape Fear point and circle the island to get to Southport where he could have additional means of escape," Dutton said.

"We're getting occasional blips on the radar

screen," Hawkins said, "but they're not consistent."

"He's too close to the water," Ryan commented, reflecting his SEAL expertise.

"There's a brief flash that suggests he's now heading north," Hawkins said a moment later. "I'll direct some boats in that direction."

"North?" Dutton wondered. "Is there access to the Bald Head Island marshes from the ocean?"

"Not according to my charts," Hawkins replied. "Unless he knows something we don't."

Del spoke up. "I checked the place where the women found me, and was surprised how close it is from the ocean to fingers of water in the marshes that cover much of the upper half of the island. It's only a few hundred yards over the dunes, and across the road where the marshes start."

"But no direct water access from the Atlantic, right?" Dutton asked.

"Right," Del answered. "Just a thought."

"Keep thinking," Dutton said, turning back to Hawkins and his charts.

## ABOARD THE SEA-DOO

"I'm getting sprayed," Rufus Reynolds grumbled as he tightly gripped the side rail of the speeding watercraft.

"Better than handcuffs," Ramon Montez shouted above the roar of the craft's engine.

"Where're we going?" Reynolds yelled back.

"I've got an idea," Montez said, slowing the Sea-Doo, drastically reducing the noise level.

## BALD HEAD ISLAND

The cell phone exchange was rated XXX. "What the fuck went wrong?" former Navy Commander Randy King demanded furiously, "and what happened to the delivery? It was worth a fortune!"

"Shit happens," Montez replied dully. "The Feds got the load. We were lucky to escape."

"We?"

"Rufus, skipper of the *Lucky Lady*."

"Why did you bring him? I need you to pick me up."

"He's strong. I needed his muscle," Montez whispered. "Can you make it to my dock near the Old Boat House?"

"I'm sure I can."

"How many seats on your water bike?"

"Two."

"That's what I count, Ramon. Me and you. You know what to do."

"What about your Russian visitor?"

"He'll be safe in my strong room, and you know how hard it is to enter. Call me back when you're ready to pick me up on my dock," King directed. "Only you and I know where our earnings are deposited."

"I never forget, Commander. You can depend on my loyalty."

"Who were you talking with?" Reynolds asked when Montez further lowered his engine's noise level.

"That was the Commander. He wants to be picked up at his dock."

"How do we get there?" Reynolds asked. "There's

no access to that area from the ocean."

Montez smiled. "You need to think big, Rufus. All we need to do is get the Sea-Doo into the marshes. I know them well."

"But there are dunes and a road between here and there."

"Like I said, think big," Montez said, slowly moving the Sea-Doo parallel to the shore of the island's north beach. "Look for boat masts," he directed.

"How can they help?" Reynolds questioned.

"Just do it," Montez ordered. "You'll see."

"There!" Reynolds said a few minutes later, pointing to a cluster of catamaran masts outlined by the starry night that was beginning to be invaded by random clouds.

"Good find," Montez praised. "Where there are catamarans there are usually cat-tracks. Just what we need."

"Cat tracks?"

"Yeah, they're used to move a boat over the sand to the water. We find one, hoist the Sea-Doo bow on it and drag it over the dunes and road to the marsh. We find water, and we're on our way."

"That's brilliant, Ramon. I'm sure glad I teamed up with you--someone I can trust."

"Trust is important, Rufus, and so is strength, and you sure have that. The boat's heavy."

"Nothing we can't handle working together," Reynolds announced solemnly.

Beaching the watercraft, Montez scrambled to the beach and quickly found an unlocked set of wheels next to a Hobie catamaran. He rolled it to the shore where the beach Sea-Doo was gently rolling in the surf. Positioning the cat tracks, comprised of two pneumatic tires joined by a heavy axel, under the hull, Montez and Reynolds strained to hoist the front of the Sea-Doo onto the carrier.

"Whew, it's a heavy bitch," Reynolds exhaled, collapsing on the sand to catch his breath.

"Our passport to freedom," Montez assured. "Now we start pulling," he said, grabbing the heavy towrope. "Off to the marsh!"

With strenuous effort, the pair slowly moved their load across the beach and low dunes before reaching the blacktop road. Pausing to rest in a cluster of tropical vegetation, they quietly watched a pair of electric carts pass. When no one else was in sight, they pulled their conveyance over the road into foliage on the other side, just in time to avoid detection by another cart that faintly illuminated the roadway with its low-beam headlights. After another brief break they resumed pushing and pulling their equipment into the marsh.

"Sure hope them gators are somewhere else tonight," Montez said as the pair repeatedly slipped in the thick muck.

"Alligators!" Reynolds exclaimed.

"Yeah," Montez confirmed, "so we need to move quickly to reach water. Fortunately the tide's rising, and I believe I can see water ahead. Keep pulling."

Minutes later, a stream of water was reached, enough to float the Sea-Doo off its transport.

"We made it!" Reynolds rejoiced.

"Couldn't have done it without you," Montez said, preparing to climb onto the seat of the watercraft that was now floating freely in the rising water.

"Now we pick up the Commander, right?" Reynolds asked.

"He's expecting to be picked up, Rufus. But, you notice we only have two seats."

"Yeah, I was wondering about that, and what are you doing waving that gun!" A panicked expression of recognition filled Reynold's face as his eyes focused on the pistol aimed at his head.

"Sorry, partner, afraid your ride's over," Montez coldly replied.

"NO!" Reynolds screamed a split second before the muzzle of Montez's nine millimeter Sig Sauer flashed. The impact of the powerful round crashing between his eyes knocked Reynolds back onto the Cat Tracks.

"Sorry, amigo," Montez muttered, starting the Sea-Doo engine. "Life's a bitch, isn't it? But think of your generosity--alligators need to eat too," he ruminated as he headed towards Commander King's dock.

## Chapter Thirty

ABOARD THE COMMAND BOAT

DEA SAC Hawkins briefed his associates: "The second drone spotted some movement in the east end of the marshes, and what looked like a gunshot flash. It's being moved closer for a better look."

"Bet Montez found a way to get his Sea-Doo there," Del remarked. "I told you it's only a short distance."

Dutton nodded to Ryan, then addressed Del. "Yes, you did. You could be right. Why don't I ever listen to you?"

Del smiled. "Guess I'm hard to believe. I'm only guessing, of course.'"

"We'll know in minutes," Hawkins interjected.

"If he did make it into the marshes, where would he go?" Dutton questioned.

Hawkins studied his maps again. "If he in fact reached the canal system in the marshes he could get all the way to Southport and the Cape Fear River. Where we have a SEAL RIB idling," he added with obvious satisfaction.

"RIB?" Del queried.

"Rigid Inflatable Boat," Ryan clarified. "Great SEAL work boat that I spent lots of time on. Can carry plenty of personnel and weapons--fast and furious."

"How fast?" Del asked.

"Forty plus knots," Ryan replied.

"Weapons?" Dutton wondered.

Ryan chuckled. "When I said furious, I wasn't kidding. M-60 and .50 caliber machine guns to start, plus side arms. We're talking serious business."

Hawkins emitted a rare smile. "How about we unleash that beast eastwards and trap the Sea-Doo, providing the drone verifies its presence?"

"Sounds like a good game plan," Dutton affirmed.

"You know what's in the middle, don't you?" Del said, peering at a map of Bald Head Island. "Commander King's dock is next to the historic Old Boat House. Bet that's where the Sea-Doo is heading."

"Damn, you could be right," Dutton conceded.

"Look at the monitor," Hawkins directed. "The drone's right over the Sea-Doo. The picture's good, but it's clouding up and beginning to mist a bit, so we don't know how long our aerial surveillance will last."

"Clear enough for now," Dutton said, "but there's only one person on the boat. Weren't there two the last time we saw it?"

"Looks like it's only Ramon Montez now," Ryan said. "What happened to Reynolds?"

"One of the secrets of Old Baldy?" Del questioned.

*  *  *

Former Commander Randy King was in his safe room with Russian Colonel Serge Petrov, explaining what had gone wrong on the drug delivery. The Russian listened with escalating rage. "You mean the entire shipment was lost, and the submarine too! Disaster! How could this happen?"

"You know there are always risks, Serge, but don't worry, your payment is assured. All I have to do is get to my strongbox on the mainland where there are plenty of funds to pay you. Ramon is on the way here to ferry me there. You'll be secure here in my reinforced room until I return. The Feds will quickly cease looking for us. All they want is the shipment, and the publicity."

"Don't forget my sub."

"We'll recoup the loss on the next load, Serge. You know the demand for our product just keeps increasing. We just have to keep the faith. Now, I have to hurry to meet Ramon. Relax, and don't let anyone else enter. As you know, the entrance optical scanner can only work with my eyes."

\*\*\*

Hawkins took a call from the 33-foot Customs fast boat that idled just off the Shoals sandbar. He listened attentively, nodding understanding before addressing his colleagues. "The boat they dispatched to the shoal with a search and arrest party is wrapping up their work. Customs will take custody of the cocaine and the sub crew."

"Any problems?" Dutton asked.

Hawkins grinned. "Not from the sub crew that will be shipped back to Colombia, but the Captain, Alvarez, tried to escape."

"And?"

"We have an unlikely hero. You know the retired Customs agent who went along for the ride?"

"Yeah, my old associate, Chuck Phillips,'" Dutton replied.

"Well, Alvarez pulled out a hidden pistol and got

the drop on the arresting party that had moved to the shoal. He hopped into their boat, ready to take off."

"Go on," Dutton urged.

"Your old buddy grabbed a conch shell on the sand and heaved it at Alvarez, knocking the gun from his hand--a blazing fast ball."

"Yeah, that reminds me that Chuck was a star pitcher on the law enforcement interleague team. Sonofagun. Good for him."

"That's not all," Hawkins continued. "He also launched himself head first at the Captain, knocked him down, and slapped on handcuffs another agent handed him."

Dutton laughed. "Sounds just like Chuck. He was always impetuous. I'll have to buy him a case of his favorite brew. What a guy!"

"What about Beau Chamberlin?" Ryan asked.

"Customs will confiscate the *Lucky Lady,* and the locals have filed a batch of charges against him, in addition to the Federal counts. He won't be doing any fishing for a long time," Hawkins, concluded.

"That leaves us with some serious business on Bald Head Island," Dutton asserted.

"Time for us to earn our pay. How do we get there?"

"Courtesy of the Bald Head Island Department of Public Safety," Hawkins replied. "Chief Martin is waiting on the island's East Beach Drive with an emergency van to deliver you to Commander King's hideout. We'll put you ashore on one of our inflatables so you and your team can join the fun on the island."

"Thank Heaven for law enforcement cooperation, Dwight. You guys did great, by the way. We'll celebrate when we complete our share."

Ten minutes later, Dutton, Ryan, Del, and Special Agent Brad Evans from the FBI's Wilmington Resident Agency splashed ashore and hurried to the nearby road where the Bald Head Island officers waited.

\* \* \*

## SHOALS CLUB

"We had a ring-side seat to all the action, thanks to you," Leigh Daly complimented Peggy Champion.

"Yes, it will be hard to top this show," Jenny Malone agreed.

Champion beamed with satisfaction. "It was kind of special, wasn't it? But wouldn't it have been a blast to be involved in the action?"

Daly nodded. "Like watching a TV show from the safety of our homes. The guys get to be in the midst of it."

"So we just sit quietly at home while they do their work," Miller commented.

"We don't have to sit quietly," Champion observed. "I think we're all too energized, so why don't we retreat to my place and continue our party?"

"I'll drink to that," Daly asserted.

"I love party," Olga Servadova proclaimed. "I bake Ptichye Moloko, Pastila, and Zefir (Bird's milk, fruit confectionary, soft marshmallow confectionary). You like."

"Let's go," Nadia Rostov urged, draining the remainder of her vodka martini.

## ON THE MARSH

"I should be at your dock in three minutes," Ramon Montez's cell message informed former Navy Commander Randy King. "Watch your step on the walkway," he added. "The mist could make it slippery, and 'Big Sam' has been sighted recently in your area."

"Big Sam?"

"The island's oldest and largest alligator. But don't worry he's probably gone to bed for the night, wherever that might be. Just be careful."

"Thanks for the reassuring information," King replied in a sarcastic tone. "I'm leaving home now."

\* \* \*

"We should be close to the Old Boat House," the commander of the idling Navy RIB said over the murmur of his muffled engines. "Any position of the Sea-Doo?"

"You can hear him coming on strong," a crewman responded. "About two minutes to engagement."

\* \* \*

Ramon Montez rejoiced at the sight of King's dock jutting into the narrow canal he had been following. "And there he is," Montez muttered, spotting the figure hurrying along the walkway that was elevated a few feet above the tidal marshland. Looks like we'll make it, he thought with elation as his craft bumped against the dock pilings.  His elation proved short-lived when brilliant spotlights illuminated the scene, accompanied by the command: "U.S. Navy!  You are under arrest!  Stay in place and raise your hands!"

"Shit!" King yelled as he was about to climb onto the Sea-Doo.  Instead, he abruptly reversed directions and began running back on the walkway towards his house.

"Don't!" Montez shouted.  "The wood's slick!"

"I know what I'm doing," King retorted, possibly his last mortal words.  Stepping onto a slippery section of the wooden platform, King skidded sideways and pitched head first over the low railing, screeching "HELP!"  Unearthly screams accompanied primeval grunts, splashes and thrashing noises echoing from the marshes, sounds that suddenly ended, leaving an unearthly silence enveloping the area.

"Sonofabitch!" a crewman on the RIB summarized the occurrence.  "What a way to go."

"It's over," the Navy RIB commander addressed Montez.  "Turn off your engine and raise your hands."

"Fuck You!" Montez shouted, abandoning his Sea-Doo and jumping onto the dock.  Like an Olympic sprinter, he raced for King's cottage, carefully avoiding wet spots, only to sight the FBI trio rushing towards him from the road.

"FBI!  HALT!" Dutton yelled at the fleeing man.

Montez's response was a flurry of shots from his handgun.  One of the slugs penetrated the radiator of the rescue vehicle, unleashing a cloud of steam and rendering it undriveable.

"Damned Murphy's Law is back on the scene,"

Ryan groaned as he tried to find Montez in his sights. Bullet flashes continued from the fugitive's moving position.

"Damn! I've been hit." Dutton shouted, falling to the ground.

Del rushed to Dutton's side, while Ryan, returned fire at the fleet-footed shooter. "How bad'?' Ryan yelled.

"Lots of blood near his lower back," Del replied, rolling Dutton over and lowering his trousers, "Looks like a bullet entry in his left cheek," he said, looking up with a crooked smile.

"Shot in the ass," Dutton groaned. "Fine way to retire."

"How could this be?" Ryan said. "I always heard you were a hard ass," he said, pressing a medicated gauze pad from his combat pack into the wound.

"Lydia always said I was a royal pain," Dutton said with a grimace. "What happened to the shooter?"

"Del took off after him," Ryan reported. "He can't get far."

"You sure?" Dutton replied with a worried look. "The success of our mission again rests on him?"

"I know, boss, but you know how he always seems to land on his feet. Let's hope his legendary luck comes through again."

"Hope and pray," Dutton answered, as he groaned again.

"We need to get you further medical attention," Ryan said to the group around Dutton.

"No worry," Chief Martin said, nodding to a second Public Service vehicle screeching to a stop feet away.

*Deep Peace* - by Sarah H. Williams

"All my officers are cross trained--police, fire, rescue, including first aid. Captain Hanson will take good care of your friend."

"Good evening, I'm Paul Hanson," the trim and fit driver of the arriving vehicle greeted the group as he hurried to Dutton's side and began examining the wound. "Looks like the slug went straight through. Nothing vital hit, and the bleeding has slowed. We'll transport him to our clinic and clean the wound against infection. Sore, but safe, I believe."

"One of my prized officers," Martin assured, gesturing towards Hanson. "Your man will be in good hands while you continue your case."

"Keep up the chase," Dutton told Ryan. "I'll be okay. Give Del a hand. His luck can only last so long."

## Chapter Thirty-one

HOT PURSUIT ON BALD HEAD ISLAND

Del could hear the footsteps yards ahead on the dark blacktop rendered slippery by the light moisture that accompanied the clouding sky. Rounding a curve, he spotted headlights of an electric cart and saw Montez stopping the vehicle and ordering its four occupants off at gunpoint. Hopping behind the wheel, Montez resumed his flight, but turned into a dead-end cul-de-sac. Reversing direction, Montez headed back, aiming the cart at Del who was profiled in the cart's headlights. Del leaped out of the way as the cart raced by, with Montez still firing his pistol, one shot ricocheting off an overhanging tree branch just inches from Del's head.

Regaining balance, Del fired back and managed to hit a rear tire of the disappearing vehicle, causing the cart to careen of the road. Montez immediately resumed his flight on foot.

Despite energetic effort, Del was not gaining ground on his target when a bicyclist approached from behind. "What's going on?" the young woman rider asked.

"FBI. I'm pursuing a dangerous fugitive. I need your bike."

"Take it," she said, hopping off. "And good luck."

"I'll get it back to you," he promised as he sped away, travelling only a few hundred yards before he bumped into a large lump in the road. The impact twisted the front wheel and pitched him head-first to the pavement, scraping his face and right arm. Stunned, Del opened his eyes to behold the cause of his crash, his right hand resting on the tubular object he had struck. It felt warm, scaly, and slimy! His eyes widened as the defused light from the low-level roadside lights revealed a large black snake that reminded him of an oversize Polish sausage. Great Godfrey! Del thought, jerking his hand away and jumping to his feet to watch the undulating creature slither across the road and disappear into the adjacent marsh.

Thank you, my overworked guardian angel, Del sighed, picking up the bike. He could detect no sounds of his elusive quarry, so he remounted the bike and headed for King's cottage.

* * *

Good fortune shines upon you, Ramon, the fleeing man told himself as he strived to discern his location and plan his further escape. He began walking in the direction of the island's South Beach, remaining close to concealing roadside foliage. Find a bike, steal a boat at the marina, get to Southport, grab a car and keep going, were his consuming thoughts. Figure a way later to recover the fortune he and the Commander had stashed away. Plan formed, Ramon Montez trudged ahead.

## COMMANDER KING'S COTTAGE

"Do you think anyone else is inside?" Ryan asked the Wilmington agent as they watched Del arrive on his borrowed bike. "The Navy crew was pretty convinced that King fed that old alligator."

"It looks completely quiet," Evans replied as a winded Del walked up.

"What the hell happened to you?" Ryan asked, studying Del's scrape wounds and torn clothes.

"A long story, involving a big snake you probably won't believe," Del responded. "I'll give you details later. Let's see what we can find here."

"Porch light on," Ryan remarked, "and some lights on inside."

"Front door unlocked," Evans said, turning the knob.

Handguns ready, the trio cautiously entered and immediately dispersed to the first floor rooms. Finding nothing exceptional, they soon reassembled in the hallway leading to an imposing locked door.

"Shit," Ryan exclaimed as he moved closer. "An optical scanner!"

"And whose eyes do you suppose are required to activate its operation?" Evans proposed.

The agents looked at each other. "Damn," Del summarized for all. "Foiled by an alligator."

"We'll have to force it," Evans said.

"Looks reinforced," Del noted.

Ryan smiled. "That will just slow things down a bit," he said, using his cell phone to call the commander of the RIB.

Ten minutes later a Navy SEAL appeared and handed Ryan a small package. "Ever faithful," Ryan said, opening the package and extracting a handful of putty like material that he formed into a strip and stuck into the seams of the closed door. "Semtex," he informed his associates, inserting a blasting cap with wires leading to a compact hand-held remote. "Cover your ears," he said, leading his colleagues a safe distance away in another room. Pressing a button ignited the explosive, shaking the building slightly with a loud blast. A minute later they returned to see a cloud of smoke enveloping the open doorway where the blasted remains of the metal door hung limply. With drawn pistols, the agents cautiously entered the safe room.

"Look at all the communication's equipment," Evans said with awe.

"See what's in the closet." Ryan directed, and Del moved that way.

Slowly opening the door, Del was surprised to see a man standing there with raised hands.

"Don't shoot," the man said in a heavy Russian accent.

"Who are you?" Del asked.

The man did not reply.

"Name?" Del tried again.

"Colonel Serge Petrov," he answered after a brief pause.

"Russian?"

"Da." (yes)

"Speak English?"

"Nyet." (no)

"Korean?" Del pursued, thinking of the language

skill he acquired at the Army Language School in Monterey, California.

"Nyet."

"Well, that presents a problem, Colonel. We have a lot of questions about what you are doing here, and your relationship with Commander King, or, I should say, the late Commander King."

The Russian's eyes blinked rapidly at that information, but he made no comment.

"Do you understand what I said?" Del continued.

"Nyet," the man repeated.

"Too bad," Del said, "and while we work that out, you are under arrest as a possible accessory to a raft of crimes." Pulling out a set of handcuffs, Del shackled the Colonel's wrists.

"Look what I found," Del declared as he led his prisoner out of the closet, placed him on a straight-backed chair and secured his hands behind its back.

"Who is he?" Ryan questioned.

"Says he's Colonel Serge Petrov and a Russian, but claims he doesn't speak English."

"Convenient," Ryan snickered with a cynical expression.

"We need a translator," Evans said, joining his associates and studying the Russian.

Del smiled as he pulled out his cell phone. After a brief exchange he disconnected and displayed a satisfied look. "Nadia is on the way, along with Tanya. They are multi-lingual, along with their other talents. And, Tanya has special expertise that might impress the Colonel. I'm certain the man will be talking freely after meeting these ladies."

The search of King's secret room proceeded with vigor, producing a plethora of data incriminating him in the current drug operation. Computer records, satellite transmission logs, and voluminous files tying King to years of drug trafficking amazed the searchers.

"Here's the name of an old Annapolis classmate, now at the Pentagon, probably the person getting the NSA satellite intercepts," Ryan declared, displaying a folder labeled Personal and Confidential. "We need to pass this on pronto."

"And here's a file detailing dealings with 'Fat Leonard,'" Del reported. "He's the Far East super fixer who ensnared a host of greedy Navy personnel in contract frauds. Our boy traveled in high style."

"It keeps getting better," Evans said, extracting a thick envelope from the file cabinet he was searching. "Keys to two strongboxes in a Southport bank!"

"Bingo!" a delighted Ryan yelled as the search continued until interrupted twenty minutes later by the arrival of Nadia and Tanya, delivered in Peggy Champion's electric cart.

"What happened?" Nadia asked with alarm when she saw Del's scraped face and torn clothes. "One of your women fight back?"

"Always the comedienne," he said, as the exotic woman came closer and began to tenderly stroke his face. "My poor detka (baby)", she whispered. "You need a keeper."

"He has one," Tanya reminded. "Where's our problem?"

Ryan pointed to the handcuffed man and watched Tanya stride over to face him.

"I am Tanya Tamarof, and this is my friend, Nadia Rostov. We have both been liberated from our cherished homeland that you and your kind have made into a sad place."

The man remained stoically mute, while his neck muscles pulsed and fast-blinking eyes hinted at a repressed emotional response.

Nadia then approached the Russian. "Zdrastvooyte (hello), Colonel. I'm the gentle one, offering you an honorable way to achieve justice. All we want is the truth, a dignified way to clear your conscience."

"Clear my conscience!" the prisoner exploded. "What do you know about conscience and honor?" he shouted in Russian.

Nadia smiled, then sharply slapped his face. "I know a lifetime of shame from what your regime inflicted on me and many of my sisters. I'm a graduate of your infamous Sparrow school, forcibly trained to surrender my body to the depravities demanded by our exalted leader."

"I bled on the battlefield!" the Colonel spat.

"And l bled on my back in a bedroom!" Nadia retorted. "Who's the hero?"

"Enough," Tanya interrupted. "This mudak (asshole) isn't going to be cooperative without encouragement."

"Poshyolnahui (fuck you) both," Petrov declared with contempt.

"Nice language for a lofty officer," Tanya mocked, removing her blouse to reveal a well-proportioned upper body with bountiful breasts straining at a miniscule bra. "You won't have that satisfaction, you pig," she said, stepping out of her skirt disclosing a black thong defining her trim thighs. "Working clothes," she said with gleaming eyes.

"You're both nothing but cheap pizdas (cunts)," Petrov shouted.

Nadia hovered in front of the Colonel. "Not cheap," she said in a reflective tone. "But with the niceties declined, it's Tanya's turn."

"You'll never get secrets from me," Petrov declared defiantly.

"We'll see," Tanya declared, turning to the agents. "I could use a little help, if you would remove his clothes and tie him more securely to that chair. Leave his shorts on, I wouldn't want to embarrass him with what I'm sure is a tiny khui (dick)."

"Suka (bitch)," Petrov cursed.

"And I need some common household items," Tanya continued.

"Tell us what you need," Ryan said, "although a .9 millimeter barrel in his mouth might work faster."

"Possibly," Tanya concurred, "but that might unfortunately result in him telling us nothing."

"Agreed," Ryan replied. "What do you need?"

As Tanya enunciated her list, the Russian began to twitch and perspire, but made no comment as he listened to the items: "ice pick, single-edge razor blades, scissors, nail clippers, needlenose·pliers, sandpaper, steel wool, wire cutters, stitching needles, nail punch, a small vise, battery-operated drill."

Tanya paused as Ryan and Evans removed Petrov's clothes and secured him to the chair with a clothesline found in a kitchen closet. The Russian displayed a muscular upper body, suggesting regular workouts, and a chest-full of wiry black hair. His black shorts contrasted with his white cotton socks.

Tanya proceeded. "I will also need a nine-volt battery with several feet of attached wires, capped with alligator clips," words that appeared to cause the Colonel to tense.

"And," Tanya went on, "I could use a small butane torch, along with a bundle of gauze sponges, plus a foot tub and a large rubber floor mat."

Increased perspiration covered the Russian's forehead.

"Oh, by the way, Colonel, for your contemplation," Tanya informed, "after 'graduating' from the renowned Sparrow school, I was selected to attend a specialized course in effective interrogations. I graduated at the top of my class, incidentally."

Colonel Petrov's facial muscles visibly twitched as Tanya turned to her audience. "You might like to leave us alone. Things could get rather messy. That's why I stripped down--don't like my good clothes getting splattered. Bring me my supplies, then go enjoy a cigarette or drink. This shouldn't take long." Taking a seat, Tanya directed a diabolical smile at the flush-faced man. "Comfortable, Colonel?"

## Chapter Thirty-two

PEGGY'S PLACE

The departure of Nadia, Tanya and their hostess to King's cottage left a diminished but lively group of celebrating women, with the notable addition of Rambo, who wandered around in a seeming hunt for his new friend, Buddy, who had departed in the basket of Peggy Champion's cart.

Enticing aromas radiating from Olga Servadova's baking circulated while cocktail and wine glasses were swiftly refilled. Anna Chen conversed with Lydia Dutton about the dangers confronting their FBI men. Leigh Daly and Jenny Miller rehashed the unexpected incidents occurring during their planned vacation on Bald Head Island. "Some peace and quiet!" Daly declared, refilling Miller's glass. "We did meet some impressive men," Miller noted. "I didn't expect to find such an attractive police chief here."

Daly nodded. "Nor a bachelor veterinarian who loves cats."

"Come get it!" Olga's accented voice boomed from the kitchen.

\* \* \*

Bypassing two well-lighted cottages whose expansive windows revealed numerous men, women, and children, a furtive Ramon Montez finally located what he sought--an isolated cottage several yards off the coast road. Visible through open windows was a small group of partying women. Approaching cautiously, Montez quietly worked his way to an open screened window where he was able to hear their friendly chatter. Mention of the sub beaching, ensuing battle and search for escapees clarified their awareness of the situation. A deep growl alerted him to the presence of a dog.

Now or never, Montez told himself, drawing his pistol and entering the cottage through an unlocked door.

The startled women stopped talking and stared with disbelief at the dark complexioned man in dirt-encrusted clothes who was pointing a menacing black automatic at them. "Keep the dog under control or I'll kill him," he declared icily. "I'm here for food and rest, plus whatever else I find that's useful. Cooperate, and no one gets hurt. Comprende?"

"Down, Rambo," Lydia Dutton commanded in a firm tone.

"You're Ramon, aren't you?" Leigh Daly said. "I've been in your store."

"You have a good memory," Montez replied.

"And you're wanted by the authorities," Jenny Miller stated.

"Correct again, lady."

"Give yourself up," Daly advised. "The FBI and everyone else is hot on your trail. You can't get away."

"That remains to be seen," Montez said, picking up one of Olga's delicacies from a steaming platter. "Hey, these are good," he said, grabbing another pastry.

"They should be, I made them," Olga responded.

"They would have sold well in my store," Montez

remarked, selecting another confection.

"Which is history," Daly pursued. "You won't be selling anything from behind bars."

"If they catch me," Montez retorted, "which I doubt they will. I know the island, and they don't. I know where to hide. Smugglers have found sanctuary here for centuries. Now, while I recharge my batteries, you ladies need to relax securely. You!" he said, waving his gun at Olga, "look in the closets in this room and find me some rope and tape. Don't try anything or I will promptly shoot your friends. I have nothing to lose," he added, ratcheting the slide of his weapon.

"Do it," Lydia Dutton directed. "He looks desperate."

"You're a smart lady," Montez said, carefully watching Olga who soon produced a roll of coated electrical wire from a utility closet, along with a roll of masking tape.

"Good work," Montez complimented. "Now, tie these lovely ladies to their chairs," he ordered, again brandishing his gun in a menacing gesture.

Lydia Dutton nodded for Olga to comply.

While Montez concentrated attention to the cook's performance, he failed to see Anna Chen subtly key her cell phone to the last-called number--Del's.

"Tight knots," Montez ordered, inspecting the bindings securing Lydia, Leigh and Jenny. "Don't want these pretty birds flying away," he jested as Olga began to wrap the electrical cord around Anna. "That's a fancy gown," Montez added, appraising Anna's loose-knit cotton cover-up, comprised of green and red Day-Glo dyed fiber strings.

"I wear it so my fiancé can find me," Anna said in a loud voice. "He has a habit of getting lost. I like him to know where I'm at in the dark."

"Hey, you don't have to shout!" Montez responded sharply. "I'm not hard of hearing."

"Sorry," Anna softly replied.

"Geez," Montez grumbled. "Just like women- talk, talk, talk. Reminds me to add another precaution," he said, picking up the roll of masking tape. Tearing off sections, he placed pieces over his captive's mouths.

"Now, you, cookie," he said, directing Olga into a chair and securely binding her, finishing with a strip of tape across her mouth.

"Thank heaven for the quiet," Montez rejoiced. "Now, I'm going to take a short rest until it gets later," he said, dropping into a recliner chair.

Throughout all the action, Rambo remained obediently quiet, with the exception of occasional low growls.

"Hey!" Del abruptly interrupted his colleagues at King's cottage. "I just got a cell call from Anna--didn't talk to her, but listen to the background." He put the call on speaker. "I think she's signaling that she wants me to come to where she is. And that sounds like Ramon in the background shouting at her."

"Definitely sounds like it to me," Ryan agreed. "Go ahead and check it out while we finish here. We'll be close behind."

"I need another ride," Del called to Peggy Champion. "Full speed to your place."

"We're off!" the spirited woman responded. "We're only minutes away."

While Del hurried in their direction, Tanya was studying the Russian's eyes at King's cottage as Ryan rolled a serving cart into the room. It was covered with an impressive collection of the requested items. Muscle twitches around the bound man's eyes were his only obvious reaction.

"Let's get started," Tanya said in Russian. "This is your last chance to tell us what you know. Do you have anything to say?"

"Otvali!" (Fuck off) the prisoner replied defiantly.

"Not nice," Tanya scolded. "It pains me to see a grown man cry," she added, picking up a single-edge razor blade. "A little nick here, a little nick there," she said, swiping the blade across his right check. "I'll try to miss your veins with my next swipe, but my eyesight's not too good."

Petrov winced as a trickle of blood seeped from the wound.

"Ready to talk?" Tanya queried.

"Never!" the man spat.

"Too bad," she said with a remorseful shrug. "My time and patience are limited, but I do want you to have a choice. Is there anything on the cart that appeals to you? Fingernail pliers perhaps?"

Petrov again spat his contempt.

"Guess that means it's my choice," Tanya said, picking up the 9-volt battery with attached wires.

The Colonel's eyes widened, his pupils darting from left to right. They expanded more when Tanya focused her gaze on his now damp shorts, also stained with drops of his blood. Tanya flexed the alligator clips at the ends of the wires. "Maybe we'll start at the top," she said, attaching the clips to the man's earlobes. "We can always proceed lower, if necessary."

Silence reigned for several seconds before a piercing screech filled the air. "Eeaghh!" resounded throughout the cottage, followed seconds later by a similar bloodcurdling scream, then a series of plaintive moans. Eerie quiet returned.

A minute later, Tanya appeared at the door, a subdued expression of her face. "The Colonel is ready to talk," she said. "Ask him anything. If he doesn't cooperate, remind him that Tanya hasn't even started yet."

Watching Tanya sag into a nearby chair, Nadia hurried to her countrywoman's side and placed her arms around the shuddering woman. "You know I hate this," Tanya sighed. "It brings back memories of all the horrid things we were forced to endure."

"I know," Nadia softly consoled. "We can never forget, but we have new hope in our adopted land."

Tanya managed a weak smile. "It is a long way from Moscow to Bald Head Island, isn't it?"

## PEGGY'S PLACE

Ramon Montez's taut nerves allowed him mere minutes of rest before he was up and searching adjacent rooms, pleased to find a loaded pistol concealed under layers of women's clothes in a bedroom dresser. Insurance, he concluded, pocketing the .38 caliber snub-nose Smith and Wesson revolver. Returning to the room of bound women, Montez surveyed the scene and made a decision.

"No offense, ladies, but I'm selecting the youngest and prettiest to accompany me on my journey to freedom. Her colorful gown will brighten the way," he said, untying Anna from her chair. "Behave and you'll live, Moonbeam," he said, leading her by her bound hands out of the room. "Good evening, ladies," Montez said in parting. "A pleasure to meet you, and compliments to the chef."

Leading Anna to the two-seat cart he had spotted in the carport, Montez lashed her to the passenger seat back and attached her seat belt. He untied her hands and told her to hang on to the side rail. Starting the cart, Montez headed down the path to the main road and turned right. Visible to the left in the near distance were the headlights of an oncoming cart.

"Hold on tight," Montez directed. "Don't want my insurance policy falling out." Masking tape stretched across her mouth, precluded a response from Anna, but didn't prevent her right hand, hanging limply at her side to be energetically tugging at the loose strings of her vibrant cover. With persistent effort, she managed to loosen one strand and rub it against a sharp seat flange, cutting it loose. Elated, she increased her effort and sections of her fluorescent gown soon began floating to the edge of the dimly lit road.

## KING'S COTTAGE

"He's talking nonstop," Ryan remarked to Evans. "Get it all recorded, and prepare a 302. Have him sign his statement, then ask the locals to jail him for us. We need to hurry after Del. It sounds like that's where the action is now."

"An Evidence Response Team is on the way from the Wilmington R.A. to do a thorough crime scene search here." Evans informed.

"Hope they hurry, Ryan said. "Ask Chief Martin's folks to secure this place until the ERT arrives, and to transport our prisoner. We need to get to Ms. Champion's place."

## Chapter Thirty-three

<u>PEGGY'S PLACE</u>

"It's unusually quiet," Champion remarked as she piloted her cart up the wooden pathway leading to her front porch. Del was leaping from his seat before the vehicle came to a stop, rushing into the cottage.

"This is why it's so quiet," Del said as he hurried to remove the tape covering Lydia Dutton's mouth, with Champion doing the same to the other women.

"It was Ramon," Dutton declared as she was being untied. "And, he took Anna with him. They just left."

"On foot?" Del asked while the other women were being released from their bindings.

"No," Champion interjected. "They must have taken my small two-passenger cart. It's missing from the carport."

"Damn," Del cursed, "we must have just missed them. I thought I saw a cart turning onto the main road from your entrance path as we approached. Where do you think they're headed?"

"The marina with lots of boats is in that direction," Champion pointed out. "He might try to get off the island in one."

"I need your cart again, Peggy. My associates should be here shortly. Fill them in on what happened here and tell them I'm in hot pursuit."

"Will do. Godspeed," Champion said.

"Be careful," Leigh Daly added. "He stole a small revolver from Peggy's bedroom, and also has his automatic. They looked like the ones my late husband carried."

"Thanks for the heads up," Del said hurrying for the front door where he was almost bowled over by a quivering Rambo.

"You're my partner tonight?" Del addressed the stimulated dog.

"Woof," the dog responded.

"Okay, boy," Del said, rubbing Rambo's neck. "We're a team. We're off," he said, following the eager canine out the door. Two minutes later, Del was pushing the electric cart to its maximum speed of about twenty-five miles an hour as they rushed down the main road, Del straining to see any moving taillights in the distance.

\* \* \*

"Now that we're alone, I think I'll remove the tape from your lovely lips," Montez said as their cart continued down the blacktop, faintly illuminated by the ankle-high, down-cast roadside lights. "But, if you start making noise, it goes back on. Understand?"

"Yes, but you'll never elude the authorities," Anna challenged as Ramon stopped momentarily to perform the task.

"Don't underestimate me," Ramon responded as they resumed driving. "I didn't survive poverty in a Colombian jungle by being stupid. Like the turtles that make it back to the sea. I should thank the nature lovers responsible for the turtle lights guiding them, and helping keep us on the road."

"I assure you I don't underestimate you, Ramon, I just want to see a peaceful ending," Anna said, while her fingers worked diligently to loosen another strand of the Day-Glo fabric.

"That's my plan, sweetie. Cooperate and we'll all be fine," he said, concentrating on the curving road.

Out of Ramon's line of sight, Anna kept pulling away.

\* \* \*

Police Chief Martin and his top aide, Captain Paul Hanson, delivered Ryan and his associates to Champion's cottage and listened to the freed women detail their experiences. Mention of the possibility of Ramon heading for the marina prompted Hanson to radio another public safety unit to check out that site. "Were any of you ladies harmed in any way by Montez?" he asked solicitously, noting the special attention his Chief was affording Jenny Malone. Heads wagged negatively, but Olga exclaimed, "I wanted to hit him in the head with a frying pan." She then added, in a softer voice, "but he did like my pastries."

"Something good in everyone," Daly jested.

Ryan turned to the Police Chief. "Your motorized van should easily overtake the cart, right?"

"No question, Kevin. Let's go."

"Left behind again," Lydia Dutton sighed as the men rushed out. She then called the island's First Aid facility to check on the condition of her husband who she had begun referring to as "my beloved personal PITA."

\* \* \*

Del and Rambo were down the main road less than

a quarter mile when Del's straining eyes spotted a glowing item on the edge of the blacktop. Closer inspection boosted his spirits. "She's leaving us tracking clues," Del said to the large Lab secured next to him by a seatbelt. "She's a wonder."

"Woof," Rambo agreed as Del kept one eye on the road, the other on the road's edge. Seconds later, his spirits were further buoyed by another glowing fabric segment. Keep it up, honey, was his hope and prayer.

"Mierida (crap)," Montez cursed as he saw a motorized public safety vehicle race by on the major road he was approaching from a secondary path. "The saints must be with us," he gloated to his hostage.

"I doubt you have any saints pulling for you," Anna Chen retorted.

"I keep telling you not to underestimate Ramon Montez. This just revises my plan. Looks like they're heading for the marina and all the boats I could pick from for our escape."

"<u>Our</u> escape? Wouldn't you be able to flee faster alone?"

Montez laughed. "Nice try, lady. You're my insurance policy. Where I go, you go."

"Reluctantly, Ramon. I'm being kidnaped, you know, and that crime carries the death penalty."

"Ha, Americanos have grown so soft, the death penalty is a joke now."

"The alternative isn't much better--life without parole -- much in solitary confinement."

\* \* \*

Montez shot Anna a suggestive smile. "That could

be distressing, unless I had a cellmate like you."

"Solitary means alone, Ramon, and I haven't heard of any co-ed prisons in the U.S."

"They allow conjugal visits in my country," Montez ruminated, pulling into a heavily sheltered shoulder area. "We'll wait here a few minutes to see if there's any more cops heading that way:'

"I again urge you to surrender, Ramon. You're a talented and attractive man who I'd hate to see come to a bad end."

"Attractive?" Montez scoffed. "Trying the old enticement technique, eh? I bet you are very successful in seducing men."

"I am not a seductress," Anna replied, as the busy fingers of her right hand kept working at her wrap.

"Well, you could be. I didn't pick you from the other women because I like your voice. You're a good looking broad, you know. Jap?"

"No, my mother is Chinese, my late father American."

"Well, your dad did a good job. Chinese, eh? You a commie?"

"No, a proud American citizen who believes in freedom, democracy, and justice, which means I oppose what you have done and are doing."

"Okay, my oriental beauty, you've declared your loyalty and now it's time to get moving again."

"Where?" Anna asked.

"You'll see. Last place they'll look for us."

\* \* \*

Del reported his progress and whereabouts on a

cell call to Ryan who was riding with his Bald Head Island police associates. "Anna's dress threads have led us towards the harbor area and we just saw a Public Safety unit pass on a nearby road. We can't be far apart from Montez. Any way to get a drone up?"

"Evans asked the Wilmington R. A. to supply one," Ryan replied, "and they're working on it, though the cloud cover and intermittent rain showers are trending against us."

"Hey!" Del interrupted, "just found another of Anna's threads. We're narrowing things down."

"We'll be with you shortly," Ryan replied. "Don't do anything rash until we get there."

"Who, me? Do something rash?" Del laughed as the call concluded.

\* \* \*

"Okay," Montez told his hostage after a short ride to a dark area bordering a water-filled marsh. "End of our ride, my Asian princess," he said, releasing her seat belt. "What happened to your gown? Looks like it's falling apart. Cheap Chinese import," he added with disdain.

"Yes, they don't make things as well as they do in your illustrious homeland," Anna chided.

"That remark reminds me to cover your pretty but pouty lips," Montez said, producing a piece of masking tape that he pressed over the woman's mouth. "Now, watch a Latino man in action," he said, leading Chen to a nearby tree where he tied her hands to a limb. Montez then jumped into the cart, drove it into the adjacent marsh through an opening in the guardrail and leaped off before it disappeared into the murky water.

"Takes care of that," Montez said, untying Chen from the tree. "Hmm, maybe I should call you glow-worm," Montez said, studying the fluorescence of Anna's gown. "It's too damn bright," he said, lifting it over her head and throwing it into roadside foliage.

"Hmm," Montez said, studying Anna's shorts and sports bra. "Nice undies. You fill them well. Maybe we should explore them later."

"Cold day, you bastard," was Anna's muffled response behind her gag.

"Now," Montez said, "without that attention getter we can resume our journey."

Rats, Anna thought as Montez dragged her away through the surrounding lush vegetation. Wonder where we are, was her related thought, answered when her searching eyes spotted a gap in the thick overhanging canopy that revealed the blazing beacon of the Old Baldy lighthouse.

## Chapter Thirty-four

With no additional glowing threads to guide them, Del and Rambo paused in a secluded cul-de-sac, no fleeing vehicle in view. "Balls," Del swore in frustration. "Where did they go?" he addressed his energized canine partner.

Rambo strained against his seatbelt and leaped out as soon as released, while Del scanned the pavement with his powerful flashlight. "Look!" he called to Rambo who was sniffing around the blacktop. "Tire tracks!" Checking closer, his flashlight beam disclosed a trail through the guardrail opening into the adjacent marsh. Nothing was visible above the marsh surface, and Del was about to turn away when his final flashlight swipe detected a slim metal antennae rod projecting just above the water. Attached to its tip was a miniature American flag--similar to one he remembered seeing on Champion's cart.

"We're getting closer," an elated Del told his partner who was vigorously searching the nearby foliage. While Del was reporting his findings to Ryan, Rambo rushed to his side, his teeth firmly gripping Anna's glistening gown.

"Good boy," Del congratulated, fondly rubbing Rambo's neck, and reporting the find to Ryan. "We're only minutes behind, Kevin, close to the village center, I believe."

"Wait for us," Ryan said.

"You're breaking up, can't understand what you said," Del responded in sporadic gasps.

Del and Rambo were already back in the cart and

underway, the dog's nose resting on Anna's piled wrap. "Sniff away," Del urged the canine that was inhaling enthusiastically and periodically raising his head in the direction of the village's visitor's center, dominated by the island's imposing lighthouse.

\* \* \*

Kevin Ryan turned to his associates after Del's garbled conversation and released a knowing smile. "Typical Del. He's close and can't restrain his impulses. We need to catch up and pick up the pieces."

"We're getting close to the Old Baldy area," Chief Martin pointed out. "I suggest we head there."

"You're the driver," Ryan agreed as Captain Hanson floored the accelerator.

\* \* \*

"Watch your step," Montez cautioned his hostage as they skirted the lush vegetation bordering the narrow path they were on. "Hate to see such a luscious morsel satisfying an alligator's appetite."

Might be more enjoyable than satisfying your depraved appetite would have been Anna's response if she wasn't gagged.

\* \* \*

Del decided to abandon the cart and allow Rambo to follow Anna's clothing scent, amazed at the enthusiasm displayed by the big Lab pushing through the thick underbrush. He was even more impressed by the obedience demonstrated when he commanded "HERE!" and Rambo returned to huddle at his side.

Affectionately rubbing the dog's neck, Del rewarded Rambo with one of Olga's chocolate-chip cookies he had stashed in his pocket. Pleading brown eyes generated a second cookie that was gobbled down with dispatch. "Okay, pal, lead on," Del directed, watching Rambo leap to his feet. "Let's catch the crook, and rescue our lady."

* * *

"Lots of lights over there," Montez said, nodding towards the aura over the marina. "Good, gives us more privacy until they give up and go home, assuming we made off the island in a boat."

Don't you wish they'll give up, dumbass, Anna mused behind her taped mouth.

"This will be a lasting memory of an exciting night," Montez continued, dragging his prisoner to the fenced park surrounding the base of the old lighthouse. "Last place they'll look," Montez repeated with a self-satisfied grin as he studied the entrance door. "Cheap lock," he said, smashing the padlock with a loose pavement brick. "Open sesame! Your palace, my gorgeous lady," Montez announced, pulling Anna through the opening and closing the door. "Cozy," he commented of the diminished light, "but with just enough light from the windows to guide us to the penthouse."

"Mmphf," Anna mumbled.

"You go first," Montez ordered, prodding Anna towards the narrow stairs that circled the perimeter wall.

Anna mumbled louder, shook her head, and refused to move.

"Have something to say?" Montez grumbled. "Just

like a woman. Okay," he said, removing the tape. "What is it?"

"I need something to hang on to going up the stairs."

Montez studied the stairway. "Yeah, I guess you do. Don't want you to fall off and break your lovely neck," he said, untying her hands. "I'll just leave the cord hanging loose in case I need to tie you up again. But, the tape goes back on. I don't want you yelling out our location."

"Bastard," Anna managed to partially mutter while the masking tape was restored.

"Zorra (bitch)," Montez responded, pushing Anna roughly up the first flight.

\* \* \*

Primed with Anna's scent inhaled from her colorful wrap, Rambo sniffed eagerly while following an unwavering line through surrounding vegetation in the direction of the old lighthouse. Del followed breathlessly behind, and five minutes later they stood at the base of the lighthouse, looking at the damaged entrance door. "They're in the lighthouse," Del called Ryan. "I'm going in. Bring backup."

"Wait for us," Ryan futilely urged, a split second after he heard a disconnecting click.

\* \* \*

Carefully entering the historic edifice, Del took a minute to adjust his eyes to the darkness, and to listen. Rambo's ears perked attentively while Del held his collar in restraint. "STAY!" he quietly commanded the quivering canine. Convinced that no one lurked on the ground floor, Del turned toward the stairs where he heard a squeaking sound on a landing above.

"FBI!" he called out. "You are surrounded, Ramon. Release the woman. Surrender and no one gets hurt." Focusing his powerful flashlight, he projected its bright beam upwards. No one was in view, but the quick survey revealed the interior layout and its series of landings, surrounding the open center of the octagonal structure.

"BAM!" was the shattering response to Del's demand, as a burst of flame from above sent a 9-millimeter slug dangerously close to Del and Rambo. "Que te jordan! (fuck you)" was Montez's defiant response.

With extinguished flashlight, Del moved slowly up a few steps, Rambo at his feet, finding the protection of a landing overhang. Deciding to try another approach, he called out. "How about a mano to mano (man to man) discussion that could benefit you? Exchange me for the scrawny woman."

"Scrawny!" Anna reflected with indignation behind her gag. "He'll pay for that!"

"What? And give up my bargaining chip? You're a carbon (idiot)," Montez said, punctuating his reply with another booming shot that echoed around the tower and partially obscured rapid shuffling sounds revealing urgent upward movement.

Del and Rambo also moved up, with Del calling out, "No cojones (testicles), Ramon? Hiding behind a woman?"

The taunt prompted another muzzle blast that disclosed his location near the top landing where a narrow wooden ladder led to the lighthouse beacons above.

From the landing below, ambient light outlined Montez and Anna standing near the bottom of the ladder, with Montez obviously trying to force her up the steps. "Move, or I'll shoot you!" Montez yelled. "I have nothing to lose now," he said, pulling her by her roped hands.

Suddenly, with unrestrained force, Rambo broke loose from Del's grip and jumped to the landing above and sank his prominent teeth into Montez's left leg.

"Oww!" Montez screamed, struggling to break free. A swipe of his gun hand at Rambo only intensified the dog's grip. Simultaneously, Anna swung the bindings on her wrists at Montez, snagging his automatic that fell to the floor, while Del leaped up to the platform to subdue Montez.

"Let go," Del ordered Rambo, "we want to take this jackass alive," he said, pointing his Glock 225 at the cowering man.

"Okay, you win," Montez said, splaying his hands out in a gesture of surrender, then suddenly drawing a small revolver concealed at the small of his back. Pointing it at Del, he pulled the trigger.

"Hostia! (holy fuck)" Montez swore when it didn't fire.

"Hijueputa! (son of a bitch)" he said when his second trigger pull failed, as did his next three.

"That's it," Del said, reaching out to grab the gun from the dumbfounded fugitive. "Five's all you get."

"Double hijueputa (double son of a bitch)" Montez cried, an unbelieving expression on his face, instantly followed by, "adios, you bastardos," as he leaped over the wall into the open space in the center of the tower. Time seemed momentarily suspended until a sickening splattering thud resounded upward. The stunned survivors remained frozen in place, aside from a sympathetic whimper from Rambo who was restrained by Del from racing below.

"Why didn't you shoot him?" Anna exclaimed as soon as he removed the tape covering her mouth.

"You were in the line of fire," he announced simply.

"The scrawny one?"

"Will I ever live that down?"

"Not if you promise to fatten me up on our honeymoon."

"Promise," he assured with a lingering kiss.

"And why didn't his gun fire? It looked fully loaded."

Del shook his head. "God's will, I guess. You'll have to ask Peggy Champion. It was her gun. Maybe it's another of the mysteries of Old Baldy."

"Well, whatever, I'm mentally reciting an ancient Chinese blessing."

"You're not the only one praying," Del concurred.

"Hey!" a booming voice sounded from below. "You okay up there?"

"Yeah," Del replied, "we'll be down shortly. Have a little unfinished business up here."

"Well, you're business is finished down here," Ryan yelled. "We almost got hit with a flying body when we walked in. Looks like it was Montez, best we can tell."

"It was," Del assured. "I have his guns, and Rambo can identify the body."

"Rambo?"

"Long story. I'll fill you in shortly."

Turning to Anna, Del said, "Up the ladder. We didn't come all this way to miss the 360 degree view of this magical island." Patting Rambo's head, he said, "you stay here," firmly repeating the word STAY.

"The ladder is kind of narrow," Anna said.

"Not for a scrawny lass," Del jested, patting her bottom.

"How about for a fat culo? That's ass, smarty," Anna laughed, returning the pat. Two minutes later, they stood on the top platform, absorbing the surrounding breathless view.

"How can it be any better?" he asked.

"With you, never," she sighed, planting a soulful kiss. "You almost died," she said in a trembling voice.

"Almost," he somberly agreed.

"I was almost a widow before I was a bride."

"We need to take care of that, Anna."

"How long have we been saying that, Del?"

"Too long, my love."

"And, you offered to exchange yourself for me."

"I wouldn't be anything without you, Anna."

Tears clouded her view of the magnificent vista as they pressed together in a stimulating embrace.

## Chapter Thirty-five

By the time they worked their way down, Chief Martin and his crew had bagged the body and collected the scattered remnants. "The wooden floor somewhat softened the impact," one aide remarked. "We'll transport the body to our medical lab and hold it for the medical examiner."

"What's the short story?" Martin asked.

"We had a couple of heroes," Del responded. "Anna knocked his gun away, and Rambo bit his leg."

"Whoa," Anna interjected as she listened to Del's report. "Montez shot at this guy five times. He's the hero."

Martin raised his eyebrows.

"The gun misfired, Chief. I was very lucky."

Martin shook his head in wonderment. "Five times? I'll say you were lucky. Well, with three witnesses, I'd say it's clearly a suicide."

"We'll follow up for the chain of custody," Ryan remarked.

"Understood," Martin said. "So, where do we go from here?"

Del smiled. "I recommend we all repair to Peggy Champion's to wind down. I need to return one of her carts, and explain what happened to the other."

"And why her bullets didn't kill you," Anna added.

"Yes, that is a mystery," Del said with a slight smile. "I'll let Peggy explain. Let's go party!"

It was close to midnight when the group arrived at Champion's cottage. A table spread with appealing snacks was dominant, next to a well-stocked bar displaying uncorked bottles of wine. A bucket of cold assorted beers adjoined on a serving table. A beaming Olga presided over the offerings, surrounded by the hosting women, Peggy Champion, Lydia Dutton, Leigh Daly, and Jenny Malone.

"We're so relieved you are well," Champion greeted. "Relax and indulge, then tell us what we're so eager to hear."

The obedient guests happily complied before sliding into plush chairs, Andy Dutton, who had just arrived, selecting one with several overstuffed soft cushions.

"Glad to have you back in action, my beloved PITA," Lydia welcomed her husband, squeezing his hand.

"Glad to be here," he said. "PITA?"

"Tell you later, dear, face down pillow talk," she giggled.

"You're getting too much sun," he said, turning towards Del. "What do I hear about you dodging five bullets?"

"Good question," Del said, turning with a grin towards Peggy Champion.

With all eyes centered on her, Champion looked down at her hands. "Yes, it was my gun, and it was loaded. It's an imposing little weapon, designed to impress opponents."

She paused, and took a sip of chardonnay. "I love every living creature," she continued, "and deplore taking any life."

"But it contained five bullets, fired directly at Del," Leigh Daly said in a confused voice.

Champion shrugged her shoulders, and cleared her

throat. "They were blanks."

Del released a knowing smile.

"I know, I know," Champion said in a contrite voice. "A foolish woman who could have cost a good man his life. What if he had needed it to defend himself?" She directed tearing eyes at Del.

"It's okay," Del said, rising and walking over to stroke the woman's shoulder. "It all worked out. I suspected that might be the case after the first shot."

The group smiled in relief, shook hands with Del and Champion, and headed back to the treats. Jenny Malone hovered close to Chief Martin. "I understand your department performed magnificently," she complimented the beaming officer who enthusiastically refilled her wine glass.

Captain Hanson chatted amiably with Nadia and Tanya who giggled at his mispronunciations of Russian words he was struggling to learn from an online Berlitz course. "You're so cute," Nadia cooed, prompting a rosy flush on the officer's pale face.

Chuck Phillips and his veterinarian brother, John, who joined the party at Champion's invitation, were avidly engaged in reviewing highlights of the events with law enforcement representatives, except when the brother's eyes wandered towards Leigh Daly who was performing as volunteer barmaid. He soon wandered in that direction to offer help.

Andy Dutton summoned his FBI group aside for a quiet business session. "We've still got work to do, gents, primarily the bank safe deposit boxes in Southport." Nodding to Evans, he asked, "Brad, you have the keys, and the local contacts. How early tomorrow can we act on that?"

"As soon as we can after the bank opens, Andy. Meanwhile, I'll contact the local Assistant United States Attorney with our probable cause information for authorization, then reach the nearest U.S. District Judge for a search warrant. Should have all that done by early afternoon, then we can see what the boxes contain. Suggest an early ferry to Southport."

"Sounds reasonable," Dutton agreed. "The boxes aren't going anywhere until we get there with the keys and the warrant. Let's meet at the bank at one."

"That should give me enough time to complete the paper work," Evans said. "See you there," he said, returning to the party.

When the wall clock chimed one a.m. Peggy Champion assessed her guests and addressed the group. "We have too much to celebrate, and too little time to do it justice. Besides, we have more wonderful people to thank, and too little space here to do it properly, so I'm inviting everyone present, and our additional heroes, to a gala celebration tomorrow night at the-Shoals Club."

Applause followed her announcement as guests emptied their glasses and prepared to leave. "Until tomorrow," Champion called cheerily to her departing guests. "Whew," she sighed, sagging into a foyer chair. "I don't know how much more excitement this poor little island girl can handle."

## BALD HEAD ISLAND FERRY

"How's the fanny?" Del asked Dutton as they sat in the inside cabin of the *Ranger* heading out of the Bald Head Island harbor.

"Tender, and my wife thinks it's funny, calling me her beloved PITA."

Ryan, lounging in an adjacent seat chuckled. "We've been calling you that for years."

"That's really funny too, Kevin. Where's Brad?"

"He went over on the first boat," Del replied. "Said he had a lot of work to do."

"Good agent," Dutton commented. "We need ones like him in the field."

"Not to argue, boss," Ryan interrupted, "but also at headquarters, as indicated by what's happened recently there."

Dutton shook his head in dismay. "For sure, Kevin, it would never have happened in the old days. What a disgrace."

"Didn't mean to rile you, Andy, especially in your injured condition."

"Wish my injury could have happened to some of those hot shots at headquarters, but let's get back to business. What do we do with what we find?"

"Pursue the leads, like we always do," Del opined. "Never know where they might lead. That's what makes this job so appealing."

Dutton turned towards Del. "You know, Del, despite all the headaches you've caused me, you're not a bad guy."

"Does that endorsement include your sore ass, sir?"

Del asked with a broad smile.

"Remains to be seen, smart aleck," Dutton said, turning his attention to the local sports section.

## SOUTHPORT

On schedule, the FBI group was entering the Bank of Southport, Special Agent Brad Evans displaying the recently issued search warrant.

The friendly head teller welcomed them graciously after examining their credentials, exclaiming, "My, I haven't seen so much interest in our safe deposit boxes in months. Another gentleman was just here this morning about those very boxes."

Perplexed looks flashed between the agents. "This morning?" Evans gasped.

"Yes, he left about two hours ago, loaded down, I must say."

"Loaded down?" Del asked.

"Oh, yes, carrying two large cargo bags. I, of course, had no idea of what they contained."

"Of course," Del commented.

"And, I was impressed with how he carried it all, what with his bandaged left arm.

"Bandaged arm?" Dutton pressed.

"Yes," the teller, whose nameplate identified her as Vera, responded. "A big thick bandage. He had to be a strong man."

"Would you describe him to us, Vera," Del asked.

"About five-feet eleven, 180 pounds, good build, brown hair, brown eyes, small mustache, about 50," the teller responded.

"Good description," Dutton complimented.

"We're schooled to be observant," Vera replied. "FBI training," she added with a smile.

"How was he dressed?" Evans inquired.

Vera thought for a moment. "Mud-splattered dark blue running suit with a gold stripe on the shoulders."

"Navy blue and gold," Evans noted. "Now for the big question. What name did he give?"

"It's right here on the sign-in card," Vera said, gazing at the document. "Ralph A. Maryland."

Dutton's eyes expanded after a moment's hesitation before he snapped his fingers and turned to his aides. "Ralph, for Randolph or Randy. A, for Annapolis. Maryland, for the site of the Naval Academy, Annapolis, Maryland--his forsaken home. Fits like a glove."

"Clever deduction," Del averred. "You old guys still have something to offer."

Dutton grinned. "Maybe you young pups might learn how things got done in the old days. Now, let's see what's in the boxes."

## Chapter Thirty-six

"Son of a bitch!" was the mildest epithet uttered when the first large safe deposit box was opened with the two required keys.

"It's empty!" Evans exclaimed.

"Wondered why it felt so light," Vera quietly commented.

With growing apprehension, the second box was opened with similar negative findings. Frustrated looks filled the room as questioning eyes roamed.

"Too little, too late," Dutton wearily acknowledged. "Which means we now have a fugitive at large with an unknown amount of money." Addressing Evans, Dutton said, "Brad, check out all the local medical facilities that might have treated a man with an injured left arm last night. Del, get out an APB on our subject. Our chase continues."

\* \* \*

They reconvened an hour later in a borrowed office at Southport Police Headquarters.

"Got a BOLO out, boss," Del was reporting to Dutton when a smiling Evans walked in. "Good luck," he said. "Had an immediate hit at the ER. I talked with the young intern on duty last night. He said a man of King's description came in close to midnight with a bloody bandage covering his left arm. Said he was bitten by a vicious dog. Must have been a really big and vicious dog with very sharp teeth, the doc remarked. His hand was pretty chewed up, with additional damage running up his arm. He had to amputate the guy's left pinky. Gave him pain med, a tetanus shot, and told him to get early attention from a cosmetic surgeon. He gave the same name he used at the bank, paid in cash, and gave no address, saying he was traveling."

Dutton looked at Evans. "Ask the locals to check all lodging places in the area to see if anyone recognizes him as a guest, although I suspect he's long gone."

"We need to publicize him," Del observed.

Dutton nodded, and smiled. "Good thinking, Del. I'd say he's a perfect candidate for the Ten Most Wanted Fugitive's Program."

"Yeah," Evans quickly agreed. "Great old program. What's the criteria again?"

"Armed and dangerous, charged with a serious crime, colorful personal characteristics that might catch the public's attention," Dutton replied.

"Well, he certainly fits all those," Del said. "How do we proceed?"

"Quickly," Dutton went on. "Furnish headquarters with a short summary of his crime, his description, and best available photograph. Ident can supply his fingerprint classification."

"How long will it take?" Evans wondered.

"Depends on the priority headquarters gives it. I've seen it done overnight, like when two agents were killed in Washington by an escaped bank robber, but I doubt it would be that fast."

"What if they don't have room on the list?" Del asked.

Dutton laughed. "They once had eleven names on the FBI Top Ten list."

"How did they do that?" Evans wondered.

Dutton released a sage smile. "Because J. Edgar Hoover said to. His word was law."

"How come you know so much about the Top Ten Program?" Del pressed with curiosity.

Dutton rubbed his graying temples. "I had an uncle who ran the program for several years, and he often regaled us with its history. It was started in 1950, you know, and became a highly successful publicity campaign between the public and the FBI, netting hundreds of dangerous criminals with private citizen cooperation. People placed on the list had their photos and descriptions plastered in thousands of locations across the country, every law enforcement department, post office, and a host of other cooperative locations. Television and radio spots provided vast coverage, so a fugitive had few places to hide."

\* \* \*

Dutton paused with a smile. "One guy, publicized as smoking Marlboro cigarettes, drinking Budweiser, and driving Ford cars, was in a Pittsburgh bar drinking a Bud, and smoking a Marlboro, with his Ford Taurus parked in front, when his picture appeared on the TV screen in front of him. He reportedly felt so harried, he turned himself in, saying he was a nervous wreck. That was a rare one, though. It usually took a lot of tough investigative work to capture a Top Ten fugitive, and frequent gun battles to end a chase. But citizen tips also proved invaluable, and J. Edgar regularly touted that as laudatory examples of what he often described as the backbone of effective law enforcement--cooperation"

"Yeah," Dutton reflected, "Uncle Jim told us about some of the more memorable Top Ten's he put on the list, like James Earl Ray, the killer of Martin Luther King, and Joseph Corbett Jr., the kidnapper of Adolph Coors, along with the first woman on the List, Ruth Eisemann-Schier, kidnapper of Barbara Mackle, who was buried alive in an underground box in Georgia. The coffin-like repository where the twenty-year-old woman was imprisoned for over three days was located by Agents who dug her out alive just in time. Despite that happy ending, the Bureau got some criticism for putting a woman on the List. Other critics previously complained that there were no women listed. Damned if you do, damned if you don't, but we all know that old song and dance.

"Anyway, my uncle, who was a bit of a risk-taker and sometimes reminds me of Del, reveled in directing the Program, and working closely with J. Edgar who loved the good publicity and personally approved each addition."

"'Sounds like your uncle had an interesting job", Ryan commented.

"Oh, definitely," Dutton continued, "He was involved for years in all of the Bureau's public relations endeavors, ranging from special behind-the-scenes tours of headquarters to writing books and making television shows and movies. 'And they're paying me for this!' he often joked. He was a colorful old Bureau character of the walk-through-the-walls era agent, thoroughly dedicated to Hoover's unapologetic battle against crime and communism, and commitment to keeping the grubby hands of politicians off his beloved agency."

"Oh, for the good old days," Evans observed with a chuckle, "and thanks for the history lesson. The Top Ten list has really produced great results. I hope we have similar luck in catching our guy, but I doubt he will give up easily."

"I concur," Dutton said. "So, Brad, since I assume your Special Agent in Charge in Charlotte will designate you case agent in this fugitive hunt, I suggest you submit the necessary data ASAP."

"Will do, Andy. I'll drive home to Wilmington tonight, and get on it first thing in the morning. Then what?" Evans asked.

Dutton eyed his team. "Hope and pray, while Del and Kevin get this old PITA back to Bald Head Island."

## BALD HEAD ISLAND

Everyone slept in the morning after with a few of the women devoting time to enjoy the sunny beach. The men gathered in Dutton's rental cottage to pursue business.

Evans called from Wilmington to report that he had submitted King's recommendation to become a member of the Ten Most Wanted Fugitive's list. "No results on the APB," he added.

"Thanks, Brad. See you tonight. Be sure all our involved associates are invited."

"Roger that, I almost forgot to tell you, NCIS and a Bureau agent arrested the Navy Captain contact of King at the Pentagon late yesterday."

"How did it go down?"

"Initial shock and denial, but as soon as they enumerated the evidence the guy collapsed completely and started spilling his guts. Said he always considered King a loose cannon. Real loyalty."

Disconnecting, Dutton informed Del and Ryan of the Pentagon action and summarized the situation. "Well, despite knowing that a prime subject is at large with potentially a load of money, we need to remember the substantial seizure--close to a half billion dollars worth of cocaine kept off our streets."

"Don't forget the new model Russian drug sub," Ryan observed. "We had a couple of wins, but the battle goes on."

"I wonder how much was in those safe deposit boxes," Del pondered.

"Probably a lot more than was found in the Maryland bank boxes that Anna came into," Ryan commented. "What was that total?"

"At least a million," Del replied, "but possibly double that, depending on who the courts decide is the rightful heir to the other million."

"Yeah," Ryan recalled, "didn't we call her the million-dollar baby, and advise everyone to treat her right? I hope you're doing that, Del."

"Trying to, Kevin. But you know it's not the money why I love her."

"We know that, Del, but you're sure taking your time to ring the wedding bells."

"Yes," Del agreed. "You're absolutely right, but something always seems to happen, to defer the big day."

"Don't miss the boat," Dutton added to the discourse as the trio answered Olga's call for lunch. "Come get my goulash. It good."

*  *  *

Sleepy eyes indicated afternoon naps for most of the group, but Del eyed the selection of bicycles parked at the cottage entrance and suggested that he and Anna take a bike ride. Fifteen minutes later they were resting near an ocean dune, listening to the soft lapping of gentle waves washing up on the sandy shore.

"How many more near misses do we have?" Anna murmured wistfully to Del, sprawled on the nylon jacket he had spread on the sand.

"We were blessed again, Anna. That gun sure looked deadly."

"And you offered to exchange yourself for me, Del. Are your nine lives running out?"

"Hope there's a few left, honey. We might need them."

"We?"

"Yes, you and me."

"Like husband and wife?"

"Of course. We've been planning on that for quite a while."

"I'd say, but something always seems to intervene."

"That has to change, Anna."

"Funny, I had the same thought."

"We need to set a date."

"That might be a nice conclusion to our engagement, which I note has been rather informal."

Del nodded agreement, and released an embarrassed grin. "I know, I've been too busy doing crazy things to give you an engagement ring."

Anna gazed at her left hand and smiled. "Oh, I almost didn't notice."

Del laughed. "I know. I'm guilty, and it's not just because I'm half Scottish."

"A cigar band will do," Anna said quietly.

"I'm not <u>that</u> cheap," Del said.

"I know, my dear. You're one of the most generous men I've known."

Del paused with an uncomfortable expression on his face. "There's been something bothering me."

Anna looked concerned. "About me, us? My past? Whatever it is, let's discuss it. There should be no secrets between us."

"It might be silly of me," Del stammered, "but it's about money--yours. It might appear I'm marrying you for your money. You are a millionaire, you know."

Anna shook her head. "Oh, you nut. You <u>are</u> being silly. You know I'm not interested in the money. What's mine is yours. You are my wealth."

With a mixed expression of relief and humor, Del said, "Does that mean you'd settle for a cigar band?"

Anna laughed. "Sure."

Del laughed in return. "I always knew you were a good sport, but I believe we can do better than that," he continued, reaching into his pocket and extracting a small blue velvet box that he presented to Anna. "How about this?"

With a surprised look, Anna slowly opened the box to gaze at a brilliant sparkling diamond ring. "Oh, Del!" she exclaimed with tearing eyes. "It's gorgeous!"

"It was my grandmother's," Del said. "My mother gave it to me after she met you in Buffalo--you know, when I got shot. My folks came from Connecticut when it looked like I might croak. You remember meeting them?"

"Oh, I certainly remember those wonderful people. They were special."

"They thought the same about you."

"And you had the ring all this time?"

"Well, not long after. My mother sent it to me when I was recuperating at that beach house in Virginia Beach, and you were taking care of me."

"You mean when I got kidnapped by that monster, and we almost drowned in the Chesapeake Bay when our catamaran capsized in a storm?"

"Yeah, we've shared some close calls, honey. Someone up there is looking after us."

"I couldn't agree more, Del. I say a lot of prayers of thanksgiving."

"I think my mother was sending a message, even though she pointedly refrained from suggesting my decision. Then, something grabbed my attention and I got involved in another case."

"And with another woman," Anna remarked. "Remember the sexy blonde--your old girlfriend in Jackson, Mississippi?"

Del slowly nodded agreement. "Estelle is a nice girl."

"I'm sure she is, or you wouldn't have been involved with her. She was in your life when we met in the FBI's SHARKS special. She expected to marry you."

"Then we met," Del said.

"Yes, and you freed me from slavery, and looked after me while I recovered from that horrible automobile accident in New Jersey." Anna's eyes misted again. "You are my savior."

"I'm completely yours," Del proclaimed in an effort to regain positive dialogue. "Estelle is history, but we remain friends. She has a beautiful voice, outstanding in her church choir, and has an overprotective father. She proudly proclaimed that she was probably the only twenty-one-year-old virgin in the State of Mississippi. And, for the record, I didn't change that status during our relationship."

"You are an exceptional man," Anna commented before continuing. "How about that New York singer who plucked you out of that tree in California? She seemed hot and heavy for you."

Del gulped. "Kerry Vita. She saved my life. She was a band singer in Greenwich Village. She also had a great voice."

"Singers seem to be attracted to you," Anna said. "What about Janice, your FBI partner in San Francisco? Did she sing too?"

"Gee, I don't remember."

"She clearly had designs on you, as she demonstrated in that mountain cabin hot tub in the LUCKY DAZE investigation."

"From which we all emerged alive, you should recall since you were there. Another near disaster we survived. I assure you again, I'm totally and completely yours."

"And that brings us to the Russian hussy in the SPYTRAP special. How do you explain her?"

Del displayed a serious expression. "Happy to clear the air. I know it's been bugging you. You know I was dumped in a cellar in Maryland by Russian thugs, then joined by Nadia who was also a prisoner. We were both scheduled to be killed. Meanwhile, I was worried sick about you operating undercover for the FBI to trap that crooked Congressman. Nadia and I were both rescued by Tanya, who teamed up with Nadia to help us escape. Somehow, we all survived, with everyone performing heroically, including Nadia."

Anna displayed an understanding smile. "Two beautiful women you succeeded in convincing to defect from their native land. Quite a salesman, who always seems to end up in loving arms."

Del shrugged. "Can't help what happens."

Anna moved closer and embraced Del. "Forgive me for sounding insecure. You're just so important to me, and I feel very fortunate."

"I'm the fortunate one, Anna, just a displaced Connecticut Yankee blessed with dumb luck."

Anna threw her arms around Del's neck. "Maybe that's why I love you so much, you loveable goof."

"Does that mean you will marry me?"

"You bet," Anna said watching intently as Del slipped the diamond on her ring finger. "Won't the girls be impressed. It's really jazey."

"Don't you mean jazzy?"

"I mean all that jazz, my love," she said, as their lips met in a passionate kiss.

## Chapter Thirty-seven

SHOALS CLUB

"Hey, sounds like a party," Ryan proclaimed as Dutton's electric cart approached the impressive Shoals Club, perched regally over the Cape Fear Point. Lively music filled the evening air as the silent cart coasted to a stop at the entrance. "Dixieland?" Dutton speculated, helping his wife out of her seat.

"I like," Olga Servadova announced, clapping her hands. "Makes me feel like dancing."

"Perhaps we can show them what a real Russian dance is," Nadia said, winking to Tanya who nodded enthusiastically.

Rambo barked agreement, watching Peggy Champion's cart glide to a stop next to them.

"Like?" she asked. "I hired them from a gig at Mojo's. They can play anything. Let's see what is going on inside," she invited, leading the group up the wooden ramp.

*When The Saints Come Marching In* greeted the guests as they entered the main dining room. Red, white and blue balloons hung from the sturdy rafter beams.

"They're *The Dixiecats*," Champion informed, "a bunch of old pros who entertain in local spots."

Rollie, the graying bandleader, displaying a straw boater, momentarily lowered his glistening brass trumpet and acknowledged the arrivals before resuming a roaring welcome. Benjy, a tall, thin African-American, lovingly nursed his worn saxophone. The bandleader then tipped a shoulder to Wendall, a short, stout banjo player, wearing a red, white, and blue straw hat who energetically strummed a few bars before nodding to Vic, a heavily bearded drummer in a shimmering silver T-shirt. Vic proceeded to pound with enthusiasm on his array of drums, finishing with shattering whacks at his cymbals. Attention then focused on a wiry Hispanic-appearing man with a neatly trimmed goatee, balancing a towering bass that he steadily plunked. "That's Beats," the bandleader announced. "He keeps the rhythm and all of us in synch. We'd be all over the map without him." Nodding, with a wide smile, Beats produced a thumping range of notes. The entire band then turned towards the piano where a grandmotherly looking woman with pure silver hair, wearing a bright red dress, gently ran her fingers over her keyboard before suddenly shouting with a southern drawl, "We're here to entertain you!" She then vigorously punched her flying fingers onto the keys to conclude the introductions. With a broad smile, the woman said, "I'm Whitey, the brains of this rowdy bunch. Direct any complaints to me. Meanwhile, relax and enjoy. We're honored to be with such a distinguished group."

The applause was hearty as the band segued into *There'll Be A Hot Time In The Old Town Tonight*.

\* \* \*

"What a beginning," Andy Dutton complimented Champion. "Thanks."

"I happened to be talking with the manager of Mojo's," Champion explained, "and he said they were in the area and gave me Rollie's number. The rest was easy when I told him the reason for the celebration and who was involved. They're all retired professionals, a doctor, lawyer, teacher, chef, Army Colonel, semi-pro baseball player. They do it for fun and to keep sharp mentally."

"You're a wonder, Peggy. You deserve a medal."

"I'm surrounded by heroes," Champion was saying in deference when the band struck up *Anchors Aweigh* and a group of neatly uniformed sailors filed into the room, led by a Navy Captain in full summer whites. A rather ragged group of casually dressed but physically impressive men with beards and mustaches, followed. The applause was stimulating.

"SEALS," Dutton remarked to his wife.

Several minutes later, a similar group of sharply dressed naval personnel entered the room and the band began playing the Coast Guard's *Semper Paratus*. More loud cheers evolved.

Crowd enthusiasm was running high when Chuck Phillips, his vivacious wife, Donna, and his Customs associates arrived. "Do you guys have a service song?" Dutton asked. "You folks were key players in this caper."

Phillips grinned. "Yes, but it's not as well known, so maybe I'll have John sing something later," he added, nodding at his veterinarian brother who had already sought out Leigh Daly to discuss rescued cats or something.

"A budding romance?" Dutton speculated with a smile.

\* \* \*

"Isn't this something to remember on our special day?" Anna whispered to Del who had located the bar and fetched two glasses of chardonnay.

"Every day is special with you," he affirmed, reflecting on how important their engagement meant to his betrothed, and how dilatory he had been in presenting a ring. He decided to assuage his nagging sense of guilt with a healthy gulp of wine.

Rambo, allowed into the club by virtue of a pet-friendly policy, and service-dog rating, roamed around, enjoying endless friendly pats while searching for Peggy Champion's gold cocker, Buddy who he located huddled by his effervescent owner. After appropriate sniffs, they proceeded to chase a small ball around the room.

Chief Martin of the Bald Head Island Public Service Department transported a number of celebrants in one of his motorized rescue vans from the island harbor upon their arrival on the ferry from Southport. His top aide, Captain Paul Hanson, arrived in a second van with additional guests and promptly joined the party.

Nadia and Tanya, attired in clinging satin dresses, roved around the ballroom, attracting admiring glances from every breathing male viewing their seductive figures.

"I feel underdressed," Anna whispered to Del, who stepped back to appraise his newly declared fiancée dressed in a white satin sheath of oriental design, trimmed with gold braid.

"You are the most beautiful woman in the room, bar none," Del declared emphatically.

"The girls were very impressed with my ring. Thank you."

"Its sparkle couldn't exceed your brilliance," Del responded.

"Wow! Have you been taking charm lessons? You're overwhelming me."

"Just waking up, perhaps," Del said, squeezing her hand, only to be interrupted by Kevin Ryan who dramatically lifted Anna's hand to examine the ring. "You able to lift that rock with your delicate strength?" Ryan asked with a grin, adding, with a look at Del, "Glad you finally got your act together. Congratulations."

Del shook Ryan's offered hand. "Not as fast as SEAL's act, Kevin, but even Yalies eventually wise up. How about you?"

Ryan expanded his grin. "Cynthia and I have studied your style and have agreed to learn from it."

Del turned to Anna to clarify. "Cynthia is the former Air Force helicopter pilot he met in the SPYTRAP special. She took his place when he got injured, and helped fly us over the wild Potomac to rescue the women headed for the Great Falls."

"I remember it well," Anna responded. "I was on shore praying for your survival."

"It was a happy ending," Ryan picked up, "and with your guidance might incline me to do some diamond shopping soon. Did you find a place that gives a Bureau discount?"

Del laughed, reminded that agents have a reputation of being keen shoppers. "It was a family heirloom."

"Oh, right," Ryan said, returning the laugh, "I forgot your Scottish blood."

"Touché, buddy," Del replied with a grin. "Seriously, I think you have a winner. Early plans?"

"You'll know when it happens," Ryan said, winking. "Former SEALs act first, talk second. End of conversation."

"Got ya," Del said, waving a greeting at the DEA Special Agent in Charge who had just entered the room. "Lots of people to thank tonight, Kevin. Who's the MC?"

"Behold," Ryan said, pointing to Andy Dutton who had just picked up the roaming mic from the bandleader. "He knows all the players."

After a riveting drum roll that hushed the crowd, Dutton addressed the audience.

"Welcome all," he greeted. "It's wonderful to see so many outstanding people who have accomplished so much with superb professionalism and personal sacrifice. The walking wounded are here, and since my lovely wife had designated me as a royal PITA, who prefers standing to sitting, my remarks will be brief."

The band promptly contributed an approving drum roll, accompanied with applause from the audience.

Undeterred, Dutton continued. "First, our warm thanks to our gracious hostess, Peggy Champion, for arranging this celebration, a lady who played a key role in the success of the entire operation. We are indebted to you, Peggy."

The crowd roared agreement, stimulating Rambo to contribute a series of loud barks, followed by chirps from Buddy, Champion's golden cocker.

Dutton continued as a number of neatly attired

servers circulated through the room offering an assortment of tantalizing appetizers. "I see that Wes Anderson, Special Agent in Charge of the Charlotte Division has arrived, along with Special Agent Brad Evans of the Wilmington Resident Agency who was intimately involved in this operation, that the Bureau codenamed SEACATCH." Another drum roll flowed from the *The Dixiecats*.

"And," Dutton proceeded, "we are additionally honored with the presence of Dwight Hawkins, DEA Special Agent in Charge, whose agency originated this case in Colombia."

Benjy tooted appreciation on his glittering sax.

"Of course," Dutton went on, "we wouldn't be in possession of a half-billion dollars worth of cocaine, and a sophisticated Russian-made drug submarine, without the great U.S. Navy chasing the fugitives up on the hidden shoals that are within eyesight of this very room."

*Anchors Aweigh* blasted from the band amidst rousing cheers.

"Before that," Dutton said after a respectful pause, "we survived a near disaster when a Coast Guard helicopter was disabled by enemy gunfire. Only the exceptional skill of the pilots averted loss of life, typifying the dangers they face daily. We salute you," he said, pointing to the group of Coast Guardsmen that surrounded one bearing a large cast on his right arm. Rollie, the bandleader, pressed his lips to his trumpet and delivered the opening notes of the Coast Guard hymn, *Semper Paratus*. Loud applause rocked the room.

"So much to be thankful for, so many to thank,"

Dutton followed, "like Bald Head Island Chief Dennis Martin and his fine department, and Sheriff Lyle Lawson of New Hanover County. We couldn't have done the job without their outstanding help. Please forgive me if I have omitted anyone, but I believe I've stood talking long enough, and it's time for this old PITA to sit down, gently, I might add."

Laughter followed, and Dutton raised his hand. "But," he said, "like Detective Colombo, just one more thing. You should all know that one of the major players, Randy King, who we initially thought had been devoured by an alligator, somehow survived, and is currently at large. He has been recommended for immediate addition to the FBI's Ten Most Wanted Fugitives list that can provide widespread international publicity and enlist public cooperation. So, the search goes on. Now, to your relief, one final note. Ms. Champion has signaled that the fantastic dinner buffet is ready for your enjoyment. Bon Appetit!"

*The Dixiecats* swung into soft dinner music.

## Chapter Thirty-eight

*Happy Days Are Here Again, Blue Bayou, and Beyond the Sea* set the mood of the joyous guests who attacked the appealing display of shrimp, lobster tails, prime rib, and endless sides on the bountiful buffet. A separate table offered a tempting array of sinful desserts.

While guests diligently consumed the delicacies and engaged in personal discussions, Dutton, accompanied by Ryan, visited each table to personally thank all of the participating law enforcement and military personnel. During discussion with Chief Martin about the elusive former Navy Commander, the officer confirmed his surprise over King's escape, then added, "Been meaning to tell you that we received a report this morning from a fisherman who said he had hooked an alligator carcass in the marsh. It had a trench knife protruding from one of its eyes. Could have been 'Old Sam.' I'll follow the examination and let you know of any more findings."

Dutton nodded understanding. "Guess we all underestimated King's survival skills, Chief. You raise tough characters on your island."

"Yankee import," Martin said with a smile. "Don't blame us."

"Who outsmarted one of your native creatures," Dutton retorted with a friendly shoulder clap before moving on.

As they moved away, Dutton elbowed Ryan. "I see your old SEAL buddies haven't neglected Nadia and Tanya," he said, gesturing to the table where the Russian duo were the center of the sailor's attention.

Ryan chuckled. "They live to fight, and fight to live. Everything else is frosting on the cake."

Hovering near the buffet table, Olga engaged in spirited discourse with the head chef about cooking techniques. Rambo and Buddy reclined quietly in a corner with meaty beef bones bestowed by a pet-loving server.

As tables were being cleared, and guests were availing themselves of after-dinner drinks, the bandleader tapped on his mic and listened to a banjo flail by Wendall. "Ladies and gentlemen," Rollie intoned, "we are fortunate tonight to present special entertainment, imported from abroad." A nod to Vic drew a short drum roll and the appearance of Nadia and Tanya in the center of the room. Both looked resplendent in shimmering short dresses, Nadia's dark red, Tanya's a bright gold. With regal poise they began a slow dance to the music of Scheherazade, moving gracefully in the ballet style of their Russian training. Attentive eyes followed their deft movements that ended in a demure bow. Then, with a nod to the bandleader, Nadia and Tanya began an energetic dance that incorporated some of their Tae Kwon Do movements, emphasized by the pounding beats of the energized band. Wendall furiously strummed his banjo like a balalaika, as Nadia and Tanya made Cossack-like kicks, building to a thundering crescendo and rousing conclusion that left the perspiring women limp with exhaustion, their shimmering gowns clinging to every crease and curve.

Applause of the spellbound crowd threatened to loosen the rafters of the stately club.

"Whew!" Jesse, a curly-haired SEAL with a neat mustache and shoulder-length hair, remarked to his buddy. "How would you like to have one of them with us in a RIB?"

"Relax, Jesse," said his buddy, Cliff. "If the Navy thought it a good idea, they would have issued us one."

"I wonder about you sometimes, partner, but excuse me while I get that sexy brunet something to drink."

"Not bad thinking, buddy. That tall blonde looks thirsty too," the fellow SEAL said, hurrying to catch up.

"Well, wasn't that something?" Leigh Daly said to her tablemates, Jenny Malone, the attentive veterinarian, John Phillips, and Chief Martin who continued to be responsive to Malone's every need.

"The piano music reminds me of your playing," Malone said to Daly, "Like that Yale drinking song that helped Dell out of his fog."

Daly smiled. "It seems so much has happened since then, but yes, it seemed to work."

Malone ran her fingers over the tablecloth. "Don't you think everyone would enjoy an encore while we're in the musical mood?"

Daly shrugged. "I could use a singer," she began, then stopped and looked at Phillips. "I've been told you have a great voice."

Phillips returned a modest grin. "It's mostly at rallies for wounded warriors."

"Of which, we have several," Daly noted. "They're in this room. Let's add to their entertainment."

"Why not?" Phillips said, jumping up and grabbing

Daly's hand to lead her to the piano.

Del reminded Anna. "She and her friend picked me off the beach," he said, before directing attention to the pair preparing to perform. The man's surprisingly vibrant voice rising above Daly's delicate key touch hushed the room and Phillips sang:

> *To the tables down at Mory's*
> *To the place where Louie dwells*
> *To the dear old Temple bar we love so well*
> *Sing the Whiffenpoofs assembled with their*
> *glasses raised on high and the magic*
> *of their singing casts its spell*

The pleasing pair joyfully delivered the remainder of the song and as the last verse faded serenely away, the rapt audience rewarded the rendering with warm applause. Del gulped with nostalgia, commenting to Anna, "Brings back good memories."

Phillips embraced his accompanist and whispered, "We need to do this more often."

"You have my number," Daly replied, heading back to their table.

The band began a medley of patriotic songs, starting with *It's A Grand Old Flag*.

"We're a patriotic bunch," said the silver-haired pianist on her mic, "but we're not politically correct," she added, leading the band in a rousing rendition of *Dixie*.

Hearty applause followed, and didn't lessen when the bandleader grasped his trumpet, apologized for the earlier oversight, and began blasting out the *Marine*

*Corp Hymn.* For good measure, the band played the venerable *Army Hymn*, before concluding with *God Bless America.*

After a short break, Dutton returned to the bandstand and picked up the mic. "What a memorable night," he declared, "and how fortunate we were to be entertained by this extraordinary group of musicians." He pointed to Rollie, the leader, who pursed his lips and blew the opening notes of *You'd Be So Nice To Come Home To.* Benjy then blew softly into his saxophone, *Thanks For The Memories.* Wendall heartily strummed *Yankee Doodle Dandy* on his banjo, prompting Rambo to jump up and rush to Del's side, rekindling the bond established in previous cases. The drummer, Vic, followed with a stomping rendition of Gene Krupa's *Drumboogie,* a performance that would impress Ringo Starr. Then the spirited lady pianist, Whitey, gently played *The Last Farewell,* amplified by the resonant voice of Rollie, who sounded eerily like Roger Whitaker.

As the haunting notes evaporated, Dutton announced, "One last thing before we conclude. In case you haven't yet been dazzled by the brilliance of a shiny object in the room, it is my distinct pleasure to identify the owner, and announce, finally, the formal engagement of Anna Chen and Del Dickerson."

The crowd roared, focusing eyes on Anna and Del who stood and bowed. With a brilliant smile, Anna waved her left hand, then planted a warm kiss on Del's flushed cheek.

"May God bless them, and all of you," Dutton declared. "Thank you, and good night."

A final burst of applause erupted, as hundreds of suspended balloons dropped from the ceiling and the band played it final offering, *The Power Of Love*. Whitey sang the words, and while they fell short of the magical voice of Celine Dion, everyone agreed it wasn't bad for Bald Head Island.

Anna peered lovingly into Del's eyes. "How will you top this, my dear?"

"With my luck, I'll think of something," he assured before smothering her with a lusty kiss.

"That's what I worry about," Anna said, softly gaining the last word.

\* \* \*

Warm embraces and profuse thanks flourished the following morning as the visitors prepared to leave their memorable retreat.

Peggy Champion advised of her plans to remain in her cottage another day or so before returning to her Northern Virginia home. Leigh Daly and Jenny Malone were filled with unforgettable memories of their "quiet" vacation, plus contact numbers of a charming police chief who shared painting interests with Malone, and a dashing veterinarian who likes cats and harmonizes well with Daly.

Del and Anna huddled contentedly on the third seat of Champion's cart, while Buddy was being safely secured in his traveling basket.

"It's been fabulous, Peggy," Del summarized for all, as the electric cart headed for the ferry. A mile or so down the road, they sighted a cart emerging from a side path ahead of them. Familiar faces abounded and

Peggy tooted her recognition.

Andy Dutton and his passengers waved back, as he returned the beep and led the procession. Lydia Dutton, Olga, Kevin Ryan, Nadia, and Tanya were surrounded by luggage. Rambo perched majestically atop more luggage on the rear platform. Shafts of sunlight filtered through the lush canopy of vegetation above the road. Warm Spring weather signaled a delightful day, and minutes later the carts were parked in front of Mojo's. With sufficient time before the ferry's departure for Southport, the travelers gathered in the restaurant for coffee and rolls. Promises were made for an early reunion in the Washington area.

Anna Chen mentioned receiving word of a pending court date to finalize disposition of the assets of her deceased senatorial patron. She refrained from adding that the court's decision might render her a multi-millionaire.

Nadia and Tanya distributed business cards advertising their Tae Kwon Do studio, and issued warm invitations to visit and be thrilled. Olga reminded everyone that she prepared delectable food on the premises. "It good. Not just goulash!"

Rambo and Buddy exchanged goodbye sniffs.

As the departing group headed to board the *Ranger*, the neatly uniformed island police chief arrived to bid the visitors farewell, affording special attention to Leigh Daly.

Minutes later, the ferry was leaving the dock, its passengers' eyes focused on the distinctive features of Bald Head Island.

"Quite an experience," Andy Dutton remarked to

Del, completing a cell phone call. "Just talked with headquarters, King's on the Top Ten list. They had an opening and agreed he is a worthy addition."

"That's great," Del replied with enthusiasm, and a final glance at the Old Baldy lighthouse. "Won't forget you, old fellow," he mused before turning back to Dutton. "Sure hope the search for King is short. Really wonder where he might be."

## Chapter Thirty-nine

The Bald Head Island party quickly dispersed after the ferry docked in Southport.

Dutton loaded his crew into his SUV for the trip north.

Kevin Ryan offered to drive Del and Anna to Carolina Beach to retrieve their cars before he headed back to Washington for an inspection assignment. "Don't stumble into any back rooms," Ryan cautioned when he dropped them at the police department lot.

"I'll make sure of that," Anna pledged as they waved farewell.

"So this is where your latest adventure began?" she asked Del who was looking around at the array of beach accommodations that would soon be teaming with vacationers.

"I'll never forget it, Anna, and we need to see Sheriff Lawson who has been so much help. We've frequently met at the Hampton Inn, so I took the liberty of arranging to meet him there for lunch. Is that okay with you? Do I need to ask approval for making appointments since we've become engaged?"

"No, my dear," Anna replied with a consoling smile. "You can pursue your life, depending, of course, that it doesn't include attractive women."

"Good," Del smiled. "It could have been a short engagement. How about unattractive women?"

"Don't push it," Anna laughed. "I think I know my man who has my total trust."

"Glad that's settled," Del replied with a grin. "Now we can proceed without complications."

Anna produced another understanding smile. "There will always be complications with you, my dear. You're Del. Let's go see the sheriff."

Hanover County Deputy Sheriff Lyle Lawson welcomed the couple like family. "We've been through a lifetime of memories," he said at their beachside table. "By the way, I recommend the broiled tuna. Fresh caught. I know the chef."

"He knows everyone in town," Del assured Anna. "And speaking of that, Lyle, anything new on the murder of Captain Bill's waitress, Wanda?"

"Pretty much what I've already told you. We have a solid case against Reynolds—the DNA Kevin Ryan managed to get was the clincher. Clever work."

"He said it was a joint effort with you," Del noted, "but I just received some rather startling news from Chief Martin from Bald Head Island. He said a kayaker paddling through the marshes found a semi-submerged set of cat tracks, and when he looked closer he saw remains of a body snagged to it. It had been pretty well gnawed by alligators. You may, or may not, recall, with all that was going on, that Reynolds hasn't been seen since he was on that Sea-Doo with Ramon Montez."

"You're right," Lawson said with raised concern.

"Well, the Chief said they were able to collect sufficient DNA from the body and, you guessed it, it matched that of Rufus Reynolds. So, it seems your hard-earned arrest warrant for Reynolds is moot."

Lawson shook his head. "Isn't modern police science wonderful?" he said with a laugh. "Could have been looking for the SOB forever. Now, who does that leave apparently responsible for your abduction and attempted murder but Beau Chamberlin?"

"Yeah, the simple soul."

Lawson grinned. "Simple, but street smart. When he was interrogated after his arrest on the shoal, he was quick to give up the person who ordered the hit on the waitress, none other than lovable old Captain Bill, who has been charged with accessory to murder

*Dawn at South Beach/Bald Head Island* - Watercolor Painting by Sarah Hasty Williams

and held without bail. Lots of honor among thieves, right?" Lawson concluded with a knowing grin. "And," he added, "I have a bonus for you. I asked Chamberlin where he got his fancy watch . He whipped it off right away, said he found it. When I looked on the back and asked him what the significance of the engraved name Anna was, he wet his pants. Here you are, with his compliments."

"Still ticking," Del said with a laugh to Anna as he reattached the watch to his left wrist. He then turned serious. "I've always felt bad about the waitress," Del addressed Lawson. "She was trying to help us when she was murdered. I know she wasn't an angel, but she tried to do the right thing and ended up dead."

Lawson nodded. "Right, and she left two young boys with little help to care for them."

Anna, who had been listening intently, asked, "Who is taking care of them?"

"An elderly grandmother in rather poor health," Lawson responded, "is doing her best, but they're barely scraping by. I check on the boys when I can—good kids, about eight and ten."

"I know what it's like to scrape by," Anna commented. "A helping hand can make a real difference in a youngster's life."

Their lunch dishes arrived and lived up to Lawson's recommendation. A fruit sundae had them sitting back in satiated contentment when Anna's roving eyes fixed on a nearby table where a family was finishing their meal with overflowing bowls of chocolate ice cream. Two overweight boys were racing to see who could consume the most in the shortest time.

Addressing her companions, Anna said in a reflective tone, "We have so much, and others have so little. It sometimes doesn't seem fair."

Both men signaled agreement, with Del remarking, "A lot of things in life don't seem fair."

"I understand that," Anna conceded, "and I know we can't solve all the problems of the world, but when one can help someone else, shouldn't we try?"

"No argument there," Del said.

Turning to Lawson, Anna said, "Sheriff, I recently came into a rather substantial sum of money, through no effort of my own. I would like to share some of it with someone in need. The two boys left by that waitress seem to be perfect recipients. I know from what Del has told me about you that you are a man of honor, so I'm asking you for a favor. I would like you to establish bank accounts in the amount of $100,000 each for each boy to help with their care and education. Will you do that?"

Lawson sat back with a surprised expression, searching for words. "Anna," he finally responded, "I don't know how this guy latched onto such a gem, but he sure did. I'd be honored to carry out your wishes."

"Thank you, Sheriff, and I'd additionally like the accounts to be from an anonymous benefactor, in the name of their deceased mother, so they will have a lasting, loving memory of her. Can that be done?"

Lawson nodded. "I'm sure it can. I know the President of the main bank here. They can probably be done as trust accounts, earning interest."

"Wonderful, Sheriff. That makes me very happy."

"That's indeed generous of you," Lawson said with

admiration. "God bless you."

Del looked at the sheriff. "You see why I had to survive, Lyle."

"Speaking of survivors," Lawson said, moving to another subject, "I just received this flyer on our missing drug smuggler." Reaching into his jacket pocket, he extracted a paper notice that he unfolded to reveal a ten by sixteen- inch flyer, captioned in bold red letters, WANTED BY THE FBI. Prominently displayed was an earlier photo of Randolph A. (Randy) King, wearing the uniform of a U.S. Navy Commander. His alleged crimes were listed, along with a detailed description and his fingerprint classification, which noted that his left little finger may be missing. Anyone recognizing him was requested to immediately contact their nearest law enforcement agency.

"Hurrah!" Del exclaimed. "He's on the Top Ten. Millions of people all over the world will be looking for him, Anna. It's only a matter of time until someone spots him."

"I do hope so." Anna remarked in a moderating tone, "but it's a big world and he could be anywhere."

"One of these flyers generates a lot of tips," Lawson said. "Takes a lot of time to run them out, but you can't overlook the most mundane ones."

"I know what you mean, Lyle. We both know it's the little things that pay off."

The sheriff nodded confirmation. "Like a call I received this morning from a small local hotel about a suspicious guest who did some damage. I told the proprietor I'd drop by this afternoon to take his complaint. He said the guy left a bloody mess."

Lawson's gaze shifted to Anna, who was trying to stifle a yawn. "You look tired," he said.

Anna apologized. "It's not the company, I assure you. I just feel so relaxed after this fine meal and all the excitement. I guess the laid-back atmosphere here makes me sleepy."

Del voiced agreement and addressed Anna. "It has been a high-pressure week, and since we don't have to be back in Washington for a couple of days, why don't we spend a night in Carolina Beach?"

"That would be nice," Anna agreed.

"Wait here," Lawson said, "I need to check with someone on a few things."

"A nice gentleman," Anna remarked to Del after Lawson left the table.

"A real pro," Del affirmed. "He's a graduate of the FBI National Academy, a four-month specialized training course at Quantico for outstanding local law enforcement officers. It's sort of like an FBI auxiliary. We frequently work closely together," Del was saying when Lawson returned.

"Here's your room key," Lawson said, handing Del a small packet. "I think you'll enjoy the bridal suite."

"What!" Anna gasped.

"The manager is an old friend," the sheriff said, "who loves law enforcement. It's with his compliments. No charge."

"I don't know what to say," Del professed.

"Well, that's a first," Lawson jested. "Just enjoy."

"I owe you a big one, Lyle. Let me know how I can be of service."

"Well, since you offered, if you can spare a few minutes, I could use your diplomatic skills in dealing with an excitable hotel operator who happens to be Korean. I know you speak Korean, and could help me understand him when he gets agitated and mixes English with his native language. He sounded quite agitated this morning, and was complaining about poor police response."

"Certainly, Lyle. I'll be happy to accompany you and play peace maker."

"Great, Del. Meanwhile, Anna can catch some rays on the beach, or relax in the giant Jacuzzi in your suite."

Anna's eyes brightened. "You don't have to say that twice. Go and handle your work while I suffer here."

"Man's work is never done," Del quipped as they went their separate ways.

\* \* \*

Ilsung Park, owner-operator of the 24-unit Sea Breeze Inn, greeted Sheriff Lawson and his companion with an angry expression on his face. "About time," he said.

"Annyeong (Hello)" Del said in fluent Korean.

"Annyeong," the surprised hotelier replied.

"It took a little extra time to arrange for a linguist who could help with your problem, which my department takes very seriously," Lawson said.

"Oh, good," Park said in a much more mellow tone.

"Tell us what happened," Del encouraged, "in English if you can so the sheriff can understand its seriousness."

"Okay," Park responded, proceeding to enumerate

his complaints. "He here two nights. Pay in cash. Left yesterday. He ruined sheets and mattress pad. See", he said, displaying a laundry bag stuffed with blood-stained linens. "And, look here," Park continued, leading them to the bathroom washstand bowl that was heavily stained with black marks. "Dye hair. Hard to remove."

"Did he leave anything behind?" Lawson asked.

"Yes, here in bag. Maid kept to show you," he said, producing a brown paper sack.

Lawson and Del watched as the manager extracted items one by one, beginning with an empty fifth of Johnnie Walker Blue.

Del's eyebrows lifted. "That's what King drinks," he told Lawson.

"What name did the man give?" Del asked Park.

"It's here on the registration card: R. Maryland."

"That's our guy," Del exclaimed.

Lawson pulled out the wanted flyer he had just received, and unfolded it in front of Park. "Could this be the man?"

"That him!" Park shouted. "Wanted by FBI! He plenty bad guy."

"He sure is, Mr. Park," Del concurred. "What was he driving?"

Park examined the registration card that showed that information missing.

"Nothing shown," Lawson noted.

Park looked embarrassed. "Wife not do good job. I talk to Jieun," he said with a deep frown. "But," he added, "wife say car was silver."

"Did she say what make it was, or get the license

number?" Lawson asked hopefully.

"No," Park responded with a head shake. "She not good on cars."

"What else was in the bag," Del asked, watching as Park dumped the remaining contents on a battered desk, including several Snickers wrappers and used Kleenex tissues.

"And what's this," Del said, picking up a small card advertising a Spanish-English dictionary. The partners exchanged questioning looks.

"Gomawo (thank you), for your cooperation," Del said. "You can be certain the police will vigorously investigate your case."

Park beamed. "I happy now. FBI on my case."

* * *

Sitting outside the Sea Breeze Inn, Del and Lawson reviewed their findings. "Must still be bleeding from the alligator bites," Lawson noted.

"And dyed his hair," Del added. "And still drinking his favorite scotch."

"What do you make of the ad about a Spanish-English dictionary, Del?"

"Could be Mexico. Easy to cross the border. At least it wasn't Russian-English."

"Well, we got a hot lead," Lawson joked, "a silver car."

"Yeah," Del replied in a frustrated tone. "We were within hours. Hell, we may have passed him on the road."

"The challenges of law enforcement," Lawson commented as Del called the Wilmington Resident Agency on his cell phone and informed Special Agent Brad Evans of their discoveries. "They'll put out an immediate BOLO, and alert all nearby offices," Del was telling Lawson when the alert sounded on his cruiser's speakers.

"Fast action," Lawson observed.

"Just hope we can achieve similar results, Lyle. Anna will be surprised to hear of our little public-service excursion. And I need to let Dutton know the latest," he said, entering his old mentor's number on his iPhone.

* * *

The frustrated young G-man found his spirits spring to attention when he entered the honeymoon suite and found Anna relaxing in an over-size Jacuzzi, surrounded by a line of pineapple-scented candles. Soft easy-listening music floated quietly in the air. Clothes were rapidly discarded, and Del was soon cradling his slippery fiancée in a full-body embrace. "Slippery when wet," she cautioned as she squirmed in his grasp. "Oh, you feel so good," she cooed into his ear as they united in exuberant ecstasy. Splattered tub water extinguished several of the candles before the energetic water ballet finally culminated in shouts of delight.

"Whew," Anna sighed when her rapid breathing subsided. "Maybe you should go off on short trips with the sheriff more often. What happened? You looked so downcast when you walked in."

Reclining back in the tub with an exhausted look, Del related their findings at the Sea Breeze Inn.

"Almost caught up with him, honey. What an elusive bastard."

"You'll find him," she assured, stretching out her toe to rub his thigh.

Smiling at her exploration, he asked, "What's that behind your head?"

"Oh," she replied, glancing at the ice bucket with a protruding bottleneck and two adjacent wine glasses, "it was in the room when I arrived. The porter said it was with the compliments of the Manager. There was also a large basket filled with fruit and other goodies."

"Very nice," Del said. "Let' see what's in the bottle. Holy cow, champagne! and not cheap stuff. We've struck gold."

"I could get used to this," Anna said, kneeling before him as he uncorked the beverage, her dripping breasts swaying enticingly before his eyes as he filled their glasses.

"Better stop that or we'll never get to drink the bubbly," Del warned. "We have all night."

"And half the morning," Anna said with a simmering smile before sipping from her glass.

"Brazen hussy," Del rejoined with an affirming smile as he followed her lead.

An hour later, wrapped in giant beach towels, Anna and Del reclined on an extra-wide lounge chair on their penthouse balcony, the empty champagne bottle lying next to them. Discarded wrappers from an assortment of cheese and crackers rested nearby. "It looks like we started our honeymoon early," Anna said in a satisfied voice, nibbling on Del's ear.

"Every day is a honeymoon with you," Del replied, nibbling back.

"But we will have to return to reality tomorrow," Anna sighed, "you will resume your relentless search for the bad guy. I know how immersed you will be."

"That's tomorrow, my love. It's just you and me seizing the moment," he declared as the towels parted.

* * *

After a bountiful room-service breakfast and generous tip for the staff, Del and Anna visited the manager to express their appreciation for the outstanding courtesies.

"It was my pleasure to honor a worthy law enforcement officer," the suave hotelier said. "My good friend, the sheriff, told me what you've both been through. It's just a small way to thank you for your service."

Pledging to return some day, the couple headed for their cars that had been delivered to the hotel entrance by Sheriff Lawson and an assistant.

"Thanks again for the great arrangements here," Del told Lawson. "I'll keep you posted on the search for King, unless he shows up in your backyard again."

"Doubt that, Del, but if he does, I'm sure I'll hear from a certain Korean hotel keeper."

Having agreed to drive north in tandem, Del shook Lawson's hand warmly and Anna tenderly kissed his cheek before the pair headed for US 421.

"We'll get him," was Del's final promise.

## **Chapter Forty**

Del led the way out of Carolina Beach in his blue Chrysler convertible, after a short detour past Captain Bill's Sea Shack where he smiled at the closed sign and pointed it out to Anna who was following in her red Chevy Camaro.

Once on the road, they maintained visual contact as they proceeded slowly through Wilmington, eventually connecting with US 17, thereafter driving uneventfully for an hour until they stopped for gas and refreshments at a Circle K convenience store on the outskirts of Jacksonville, NC.

"You're a good surveillance driver," Del commended his fiancée who had managed to keep him in sight despite erratic motorists who periodically cut in and out of their lane where they moved close to the posted speed limit. "Why don't you get some sandwiches while I gas up the cars," Del suggested, standing at adjoining pumps.

Where is he? Del was pondering as he filled his tank, mentally tabulating how many silver cars he had stared at on the trip, when his eyes fixed on a motorist at a distant pump. Something familiar about him, Del mused, studying the dark-haired man. But he's driving a dark car, the agent told himself, before he noticed a large white bandage on the man's left arm. Abruptly stopping the gas flow, Del replaced the nozzle and hurried to get a closer look, but not before the black car was in motion. A partial blurred image of the driver excited Del with its possibilities as his eyes shifted to the North Carolina license plate number, which he mentally recorded.

"What's going on?" Anna asked upon her return with a bag of food.

"I think it could have been him," Del exclaimed, "although I didn't get a clear look. But he had a bandage on his left arm."

"Might there be other people with a bandaged arm?" Anna calmly asked.

"Well, yes. And the car was black, not silver," Del conceded.

"Could your desire be overstimulating your imagination?" Anna probed.

"Yeah," Del admitted. "I might be becoming obsessed. I'll check out the license number anyway," he said, calling Brad Evans at Wilmington, requesting a DMV check.

Del was finishing the fueling of Anna's car when Evans called back. "Holy smokes!" he shouted. "It's a stolen plate, taken off a Ford near Carolina Beach the other night. And there's more. The locals found a silver Lexus abandoned near where the plates were stolen, and a black Mercedes is missing from its driveway a few blocks away. That had to be him! They're putting out an APB on the stolen plates. We're getting close, Anna," Del said with joy. "Let's get back on the road. If we're lucky we may catch up with him stopped by a State Trooper who spots the plates."

"Luck's your middle name," Anna said in a calming voice, "but it's not always good, you know, so be prepared for a disappointment."

Dividing their refreshments, they were quickly back on the road, peering intently ahead for their target. A half hour later, Anna suggested a rest area stop. Del's disappointment was clear on his face. "Can't win them all," he granted, "but it's only a matter of time. Someone's bound to see that license."

Unfortunately for Del, the North Carolina plates rested in a trash can behind an abandoned gas station some twenty miles north of where the driver had spotted an excited man running his way. The Virginia license plates of a wrecked Subaru now occupied the license plate frames of a black Mercedes.

It was an emotionally drained agent who arrived two hours later with his fiancée at their temporary quarters in Falls Church. "From last night's thrill to tonight's reality," Del grumbled. "We were so close. Where can he be hiding? I didn't get my man, yet, but" he added in a brightening spirit, "I've got my woman! King can wait. I've got my queen."

"Think you'll have the last word this time?" Anna questioned with a sly smile. "Speaking of royalty, I have my Prince."

Del demonstrated growing good judgment by remaining silent. Instead, he lifted his fiancée into his arms and carried her through the doorway.

## Chapter Forty-one

MANASSAS, VIRGINIA

"Well, hello stranger," Andy Dutton greeted Del on Monday morning in the well-appointed SAC office in the Northern Virginia branch of the Washington Field Office. Del glanced around at the quality furnishings. "Surroundings you deserve, sir."

Dutton waved dismissal from his chair, bolstered by an inflated donut cushion. "Comes with the job."

"That you worked over three decades to achieve," Del replied. "You guys made the FBI we were eager to join."

"Thanks, Del. Our work attracted a lot of talent along the way, men and women like you, who are the future."

"I'm not trying to butter you up," Del deferred, "and I don't mean to patronize, but how is your ass?"

Dutton's laughter rocked the room. "Always the polished diplomat," he chuckled. "Healing, thank you," he finally replied, "just in time for my imminent retirement. I always enjoyed your frankness."

Del shrugged. "I believe I've been designated as frank and unpredictable—what you see is what you get."

"Which is rather special," Dutton said with a fatherly smile. "When we first tangled I feared you might end my career with a question mark. Thankfully, you proved to the contrary with near unbelievable achievements. Now, you can titillate another boss."

"Thank you, Andy, if I may informally address you.

You've been an inspirational leader."

"We're old school, Del, and I have observed that you are too at heart. Keep the faith."

An incoming telephone message interrupted their conversation. "Thanks, Paul," Dutton said to the caller. "I owe you one. What? How many? Maybe I can get you a discount on an airplane," he concluded and turned back to Del. "That was the Language chief at Quantico informing of a new assignment at the Language facility."

Del watched as Dutton made a note on a desktop pad before raising his eyes. "How would you like to stick around the Washington area for a while?"

"That would be great, sir, but my office of assignment is San Francisco. I've been gone quite some time."

"And a lot of things have happened since then," Dutton said, glancing at a folder on his well-polished desk. "Your file is jammed with remarkable performance in major FBI investigations like SHARKS, CULTURED PEARL, DEADLY DECEPTION, and SPYTRAP, to name a few, plus the latest SEACATCH special. You've been a busy young agent."

"I've been blessed with good luck, sir, to say nothing of exceptional guidance from leaders like you."

Dutton grinned. "Add increased diplomacy skills to your development. Remember, I'm retiring soon."

"I'll be forever indebted, Mr. Dutton. I doubt I'll encounter a better boss."

"Well, you may find out soon. I've arranged for your TDY assignment with the Language group at Quantico, that is, if you would find that comfortable."

Del glowed. "That would be wonderful, Mr. Dutton. Anna and I were discussing what we would do before our wedding. She still has a job and shared residence in San Francisco."

"Andy," Dutton reminded before continuing. "My old friend, head of the Language program, said he could use a Korean-speaking agent, either in D.C. or Quantico. Your choice. Sound good?"

"Boss," Del said, slipping back in his padded leather chair, "you have made my day, and taken my mind off my favorite fugitive."

"I heard about the near misses," Dutton confirmed. "It sometimes takes time, Del. Be patient."

"Still trying to learn that, Andy. And, Anna will be delighted so she can concentrate on the wedding plans. And, what about you? This is a fancy office."

Dutton looked around at the impressive quarters. "I rotate this grand space with two other Washington Field SAC's supervising a host of Washington-area investigations ranging from fraud to foreign intelligence to terrorism. We interplay with D.C. and nearby Maryland, keeping us plenty busy. This modern, fortified building is not far from the historic Civil War battlefield, you know, so we have a lingering sense of continuing the battle for freedom."

"I'm aware of the early retirement requirements, sir, but still wish you weren't leaving," Del said with emphasis.

"We'll be in touch," Dutton said, standing to confer a firm handshake. "See you before your wedding."

"Keep your eyes peeled for my Top Ten subject," Del urged in parting.

Poor bastard doesn't know who's chasing him, Dutton reflected with a small measure of sympathy for Randy King.

## Chapter Forty-two

THREE MONTHS LATER

QUEPOS, COSTA RICA

"Senor Nueva is back," Roberto told the bartender at the El Castillo café.

"Does he want his usual?" Carlos asked. "And is he alone again?"

"Si, to both questions. Johnnie Walker Blue, straight up. He still wears a glove on his left hand."

The bartender chuckled and winked at the waiter. "We know what it conceals, don't we?"

Roberto nodded. "Ever since I accidently spilled a glass of water on his wrist, and he removed the glove. That's when I saw his injury and the missing finger."

"And we nick-named him Senor Nueva, for nine," Carlos replied. "Rather clever, Roberto, if I might say so. Now hurry with his drink. He's a big tipper and we want to keep him happy."

Late afternoon patrons had not yet assembled, leaving the tropical café lightly occupied. Latin music smoothly flowed through the atmosphere while the customer in question relaxed at a small window table nursing his drink, leaving Carlos and Roberto to pursue their conversation.

"He always pays in cash," said the waiter, "so we don't know his name from a credit card."

"But Cate said she heard from one of her friends that his last name is Fleet. She was at a party on his yacht."

"Cate's a good waitress," Roberto said, "and gets around. What else did her girlfriend tell her?"

"She didn't go into details, but said it was a very small party--like the two of them."

The waiter smiled. "Cate's friends are varied, and they do get around. Looks like Senor Nueva enjoys a little female companionship."

"Word is," Carlos said, "that his yacht is plush, but not so large that he can't operate it by himself. Hey, he's looking this way-might be ready for a refill. Hurry, don't keep him waiting."

"So sorry for the delay, Senor," the waiter apologized to the goateed man holding up his empty glass.

"No problem," the casually dressed customer replied. "I have plenty of time, but could use a refill."

"Right away, Senor . . . ?"

"Roger. And your name?"

"Roberto."

"Well, Roberto, I'd be grateful if you could procure a healthy glass of my favorite nectar while I savor the blessings of your beautiful country."

"Coming right up, Senor," the waiter responded, hurrying to the bar.

"Another big glass of Johnnie Walker Blue for our guest, who said his name is Roger. He talks like a professor."

"Take good care of Roger," the bartender instructed. "He looks like money. Let's liberate some of it."

Hovering attention was afforded the big-spending American who eventually requested a food menu, along with a third glass of Johnnie Walker. Shrimp with rice and beans was ordered and quickly served, the meal interrupted a few times with cell phone calls. With his ears alert, Roberto overheard a mixture of English and Spanish being spoken.

Finishing his meal, the ex-pat asked for his check which he paid with large denomination U.S. currency. A generous tip generated profuse thanks from the waiter, who was quick to invite his customer to return soon, and "ask for Roberto."

As the waiter and bartender intently watched the tall man walk somewhat unsteadily out of the café, Roberto handed Carlos a $20-dollar bill. "He said to give you this--said you know how to pour a good drink."

"How about you?" Carlos asked, grasping his tip.

With a broad smile, the waiter displayed a $50-dollar bill.

"We have to keep him happy and learn more about him," the bartender declared with emphasis. "Cate just came on duty. Let's ask her what she learned from her girlfriend who partied on his yacht."

The attractive, dark-haired, olive-complexioned waitress, wearing snug white shorts and a loose-fitting pale-blue silk blouse that immediately announced she was bra-less, perched jauntily on a bar stool. She said she was happy to relate what she had been told about the shadowy yachtsman.

"I saw Raquel last night after work," she said, "and she confided more details about her visit on the *DELIVERANCE*."

"*DELIVERANCE*?" Carlos questioned.

"The name of the yacht," Cate explained. "Big gold lettering on the back of the boat."

"Oh," the bartender said, adding, "hold it a minute

while I take care of two new customers."

"Your friend told you all about it?" Roberto asked.

Cate raised her eyebrows and smiled. "Maybe not all, but plenty. It was quite a night!"

"Okay, I'm back and listening," the bartender said on his hurried return. "What did I miss?"

"Promises of what sounds interesting," Roberto said. "Go on, Cate."

"Well, it appears Mr. Fleet is a big man, if you know what I mean, and has big appetites."

"Roger is his first name," Roberto interjected.

"Go on," Carlos impatiently urged the waitress.

Cate shifted on her stool, causing her ample breasts to undulate provocatively in her silky blouse. "Raquel said she earned what he gave her--and it was plenty, mucho dinero."

"Rough?" Carlos asked.

Cate nodded. "She said she was sore for a couple of days--all over."

"Bastardo!" Carlos cursed. "I imagine your friend is glad she survived."

Cate slowly shook her head. "I mentioned mucho dinero, didn't I? I mean mucho. He invited her back, when she heals."

"And she's going? Is she the Raquel I've seen you with? Isn't she only about 16?"

"She's the one," Cate acknowledged. "Very pretty, but poor. What he paid her must seem like a fortune to her and her family. She has younger brothers and sisters."

"How did she get hooked up with him?" Carlos wondered.

"She was cleaning other luxury yachts docked at

the marina and he hired her to clean his. After closely watching her work – she's a beautiful girl with a great figure, he invited her back for a 'party.'"

"And she's going again?" Carlos asked, shaking his head.

"That's what she told me," Cate affirmed.

"Guess money talks," Roberto glumly observed.

Cate nodded agreement. "That's not all. He wants Raquel to bring her younger sister, Tica."

Carlos looked alarmed. "Tica? I've seen her with Raquel. Isn't she only about twelve?"

Cate slowly nodded, displaying a grim look. "He told Raquel he likes them young – likes to break them in. I don't think he's a nice man," she concluded.

## Chapter Forty-three

<u>GREAT FALLS ,VIRGINIA</u>

"Should we call this the Bald Head Island Last Hurrah?" Andy Dutton asked the circle of guests gathered on the expansive patio of his impressive Northern Virginia home on a late summer afternoon.

"I'm still recovering from your retirement party last month," Kevin Ryan remarked, referring to a memorable celebration marking Dutton's retirement after 33 years of illustrious FBI service.

"Does Lockheed Martin know what a PITA they made Director of Security?" Del joshed his oft-stressed mentor, generating jovial laughs.

Lydia Dutton added her contribution to the light-hearted exchange, "Now his office is so close that he can come home for lunch, I have to hurry out all my boyfriends on short notice. Never had that problem with the Bureau. They managed to keep him out of my hair."

FBI widow Leigh Daly, who had traveled north from Virginia Beach, smiled with understanding of the vagaries of an agent's irregular schedule. "You'll survive, Lydia," Daly assured. "I made it, to eventually share unforgettable adventures with all of you on Bald Head Island. Thanks, also for the gracious invitation to this wonderful gathering. I know I also speak for my dear friend, Jenny Malone, as well as our gallant hostess, Peggy Champion, who has opened her Reston home to Jenny and me."

"You are most welcome," Lydia Dutton acknowledged, "as are your companions. I feel that we are all-members of an extended family."

"Well said," Kevin Ryan spoke up, "and before we all start crying in our beer, I wish to inform everyone that I have followed Del's lead, if you can believe that, to procure a diamond ring which I successfully presented to an extraordinary lady, my wonderful fiancée, Cynthia."

"Hear, hear!" erupted amidst hearty applause.

"Damn," Dutton said with a broad smile. "That's the most he's said intelligently since I met him. I thought former SEALs were men of few words."

Ryan smiled back. "You can always improve on perfection, except when you find someone like Cynthia."

"You're my winner," Cynthia Chalmers said, lifting her engagement ring. "We got a better discount from the Air Force Credit Union than from Bureau contacts," she said, nudging her fiancé.

"My favorite pilot," Ryan smartly conceded.

"I have something to say," Olga announced, jumping up from her seat near the grill. "I don't speak English good, but I try," she said with tearing eyes. "In old country, I was like a serf. Here, I big business operator. What a country! You gave me freedom, and love. Thank you, and don't forget to come for a bowl of my goulash. It best."

A rush of hugs showed Olga how much she was a member of the tribe.

"If I may intervene," Dutton said, "with absolutely no residual FBI influence, Lydia and I want you to have uncontrolled, albeit, legal, freedom to relax and enjoy. Our home is your home. The bar is open, and the steaks are ready for grilling. The pool is heated, and a selection of suits are available in the pool house if you didn't bring your own. Meanwhile, let's remember the great times we shared, with special thanks to Peggy Champion who parked her electric cart and drove over from Reston in an eight-cylinder gas guzzler. It will be hard to match her hospitality. A word, Peggy?"

"My pleasure," she said with a gracious bow, "and greetings from Bald Head Island. Hurricane Florence wasn't far behind us, as you know, and did a major job on our paradise isle. Total evacuation was ordered, and the storm delivered terrific winds and flood water of up to seven feet. Power was out for days. Many residences suffered severe damage, including my cottage, which is under repair. Fallen trees were everywhere, and many roads were covered with blowing sand. Our favorite SHOALS CLUB was battered, but remains standing at the Point of Cape Fear while being repaired. On the plus side, Old Baldy stands proud and defiant, beaming its brilliant welcome. And," Peggy added with a small chuckle, "nature lovers will be delighted to know that the alligators are celebrating all the additional water in the marshes. That's the latest I know about the place where we had such an unforgettable adventure together. Thank you for the pleasure of your company."

Andy Dutton raised his Heineken can. "You were aptly named, Peggy. You've been a true Champion, and all of us are grateful." The warmth of the following applause brought a blush to the woman's fair complexion.

Jenny Malone then raised her hand for attention. "If I may add a note, I, ah, talked with Chief Martin after the storm, and he reported that he was all right, and that there had been no loss of life on the island. He had to evacuate along with everyone else, and returned as soon as possible to survey the damage and begin reconstruction. He said it was a royal mess."

"Appears the good Lord was looking over our favorite retreat," Dutton said, adding, "I don't intend this to be a talkfest, but I have a few additional words of recognition. We would never have won the drug interdiction battle without the Navy, Coast Guard, and all the cooperative law enforcement agencies. We didn't have room here for the entire fleet, but we're honored to have my old friend from Customs, Chuck Phillips, present, with his lovely wife, Donna, to represent all the services. I must confess amazement at how he retained the athletic ability he demonstrated when he barreled in to that gunman who had distinctly unfriendly intentions. Thanks, Chuck, and thanks to all your colleagues who performed superbly."

Phillips modestly nodded appreciation for the tribute, and the table was being prepared when splashes from the adjoining pool attracted everyone's attention, signaling acceptance of the swimming offer by Nadia and Tanya, accompanied by Special Agents Curt Oswald and Joe Moretti.

"They have attentive bodyguards," Jenny Malone commented, gazing at the foursome frolicking in the water. When the swimmers emerged from the pool a few minutes later, her eyes widened. "Where are the women's suits?"

"European style," Dutton said with a grin, assessing the string bikinis barely covering vital areas of the voluptuous Russian women.

"Whew," Chuck Phillips breathed.

"I can see why they have rugged bodyguards," Peggy Champion commented, "and handsome ones at that."

"They're volunteers," Dutton interjected with another grin.

"You deserve hazard pay," Ryan joked with Curt Oswald several minutes later when he returned to the party with a fully dressed Nadia.

"Yeah, it's a tough assignment," Oswald rejoined with a feigned frown, "but someone has to do it."

Nadia intervened. "He's one of my top students," the Tae Kwon Do instructor said, "almost a black belt, but we have some additional challenging work to do, don't we, Curty?" she added with twinkling eyes.

Sitting quietly in a two-person porch swing, Tanya was diligently trying to teach Joe Moretti the proper pronouncement of Russian words. "Sicilian's simpler," he said, sipping his cocktail.

Rambo sprang to attention when Dutton spread seasoned rib-eye steaks on the over-sized grill, a farewell gift from his FBI colleagues, then reclined to wait patiently for the bones he knew from experience were forthcoming.

The jovial participants were soon seated at an extended picnic table, enjoying the tender steaks and accompaniments while exchanging friendly banter. Sighs of pleasure and compliments to the chef rose, and Rambo happily gnawed away on a meaty steakbone, with several more being held in reserve. Grand Marnier and Bailey's Irish Cream cordials added a mellowing touch, and encouraged Leigh Daly to agree to play their adopted theme song on a keyboard, that was brought out to the patio. Sounds of The Whiffenpoof Song rose in the wood-fire-scented Northern Virginia air. As Del uttered his off-key contribution of soulful Ba, Ba, Ba's, he looked west towards the house where he and Nadia had been held captive and almost killed not many months before. Offering a silent prayer, he quickly refocused his thought and addressed the group. "Anna and I wish to advise you of our wedding date, and invite your presence."

Loud applause erupted, accompanied by Kevin Ryan's shout, "It's about time!"

Disregarding the jibe, Del continued. "It will be in Washington, three weeks from today. The formal invitations are in the mail, and will provide full details. As an additional bit of information, Anna was awarded the full amount of the contents of the Maryland bank boxes, and the proceeds will allow flying Anna's ailing mother to the wedding from Taiwan, with a nurse cousin, first class."

Clinging to Del's arm with a glowing smile and glistening eyes, Anna said, "We are truly blessed, and Del's luck prevails."

"My luck stands beside me," Del said, grasping Anna's hand. "Now, we need one more stroke of good fortune. Randy King is still at large. I've been following the search since he was placed on the Top Ten list, and we barely missed him in Carolina Beach. There have been lots of other tips, and suspected sightings, but all of them have washed out. The hunt goes on. So, we look forward to seeing you at the wedding before we rush away for our dream honeymoon.

"Where are you going?" a male voice yelled. "Disney World?"

Laughter reigned with a number of additional possibilities offered: "Hawaii? Las Vegas? the Bahamas? Bald Head Island?"

Anna once again provided the last word, beaming a brilliant smile. "In his typical exhilarating manner," she said, "my wonderful fiancé is taking us to a luxury resort in Costa Rica!"

# Other Special Agent Del Dickerson Novels

*Available from Amazon.com in paperback, and Kndle E-Book*

## *FLYING HIGH: FBI vs. THE MOB*

Adventurous FBI agent Del Dickerson accidentally parachutes into a grove of trees in California and is rescued by lovely Greenwich Village band singer Kerry Vita, hiding out from the New York mob in her aunt's isolated mountain cabin with damning gang payoff records. Tending Del's broken leg, she falls in love.

Bumbling Mafia hit men, Loose Louie Milano, and Sulfur Sal Rinalti, race west from New York to recover the records and kill Kerry. FBI agent, and Del's Amerasian fiancée, Anna Chen, frantically search for him, and a female agent is taken captive in a bizarre nudist camp. Rescuers and assassins converge simultaneously, igniting chaotic action. A fortuitous discovery by Del saves the day and he, Kerry, and Anna survive to ponder a triangular romantic future.

Spiced with conflict, intrigue, romance and humor, FLYING HIGH takes you inside the real-life world of the FBI.

## *LUCKY DAZE: FBI vs. THE MOB-REMATCH*

Unconventional FBI Agent Del Dickerson swerves from one hair-raising adventure to another as he again pursues escaped mob hit men Loose Louie Milano and Sulfur Sal Rinalti, with action exploding in San Francisco, Salt Lake City, Sacramento, Reno, and the Sierra Nevada mountains.

Major characters from FLYING HIGH reappear in this fast-moving novel which introduces new personalities, including attractive blonde agent Janice Wilson, another complication in Del's romantic minefield. The serious side of FBI work is illustrated by a deadly shoot-out in San Francisco with a psychotic killer, driving the surviving Janice into Del's comforting arms.

Enjoy an inside look at the lives and loves of memorable FBI investigators, while you laugh at the bumbling antics of Loose Louie and Sulfur Sal, and learn how the wild search, and Del's ingenuity, lead to a fiery conclusion.

### *FBI Code Name: SHARKS,* Fighting Washington Corruption

Young, impetuous Special Agent Del Dickerson stumbles into a multi-million dollar commodities conspiracy between unscrupulous lobbyists and dishonest Washington legislators. He becomes romantically involved with Amerasian beauty Anna Chen, consort of a powerful corrupt Senator guiding the fraud. New agent Lola Stanley, a former Radio City Music Hall Rockette, goes undercover as an Atlantic City chorus girl to penetrate the plot. Fast-moving action, loaded with humor and intrigue, explodes in Norfolk, Washington, and Atlantic City, culminating in a thrilling climax when FBI Hostage Rescue Team operators drop from helicopters onto a luxury yacht at sea.


### *FBI Code Name: CULTURED PEARL,* Smuggled Terror

Amerasian beauty Anna Chen holds the key to deciphering the diary of a disgraced United States Senator involved in international smuggling of precious gems and nuclear devices. Targeted for assasination by White House and Justice Department conspirators, Anna is defended by quixotic FBI Special Agent Del Dickerson, noted for inexplicable good luck until he is shot. Action-packed adventures explode from Virginia and Washington, DC, to the Canadian border. Danger, adventure, intrigue, and romance enrich this fast-paced story of greed, betrayal, and redemption. CULTURED PEARL has it all!

***FBI Code Name: DEADLY DECEPTION,*** *Murder in Monterey*

Fictional Special Agent Del Dickerson, known for unorthodox behavior and phenomenal luck, studying Korean at the Foreign Language Institute in Monterey, California, finds himself in the middle of a Chinese-Communist plot to assasinate his professor.

A Taiwanese Army officer is the prime suspect, possibly aided by Del's beautiful Amerasian fiancée. Complicating his turbulent life is the unexpected arrival of a former lover with matrimonial intentions.

A murder, poisoning, aircraft hijacking, and kidnapping generate fast moving action between Monterey and San Francisco, culminating in a dramatic Nob Hill raid by an FBI SWAT team, where Del's ingenuity thwarts the murderous intentions of a psychotic assassin known as "Scorpion."

***FBI Code Name: SPYTRAP,*** *Washington Seduction*

Unpredictable FBI Agent Del Dickerson is assigned to identify a security leak in the South Korean Embassy impacting North Korea's ballistic missile threats. He encounters suspected spy Nadia Rostov, a voluptuous Russian "honey pot" at a Tae Kwon Do martial arts studio.

While confronting her seductive designs, he is kidnaped by an ex-KGB Colonel, mastermind of the spy operation. Confined in a dank cellar, he is tortured by Tanya, another provocative "honey pot."

Meanwhile, Del's beautiful Amerasian fiancée, Anna Chen, is battling seduction overtures while working for the FBI to expose corrupt congressmen. Action rages in Washington, Williamsburg, and Northern Virginia.

With wit and ingenuity, Del survives myriad challenges, climaxing in a hair-raising rescue on the raging Potomac River featuring an FBI Hostage Rescue Team.

Non-stop thrills and chills abound in SPYTRAP, *Washington Seduction*, the author's sixth Del Dickerson novel.

# ABOUT THE AUTHOR

The wide-eyed Detroit youngster avidly following the exploits of J. Edgar Hoover's G-Men battling Dillinger-era gangsters never imagined that he would one day be on the headquarters staff of the legendary FBI Director. Jim Healy realized that dream, joining Hoover's relentless fight against crime and communism.

Following two years in the U.S. Navy during World War II, the author earned a Journalism degree at Michigan State University and applied for FBI employment. Underage for the Agent's position, he began as Night Clerk in the Detroit office while attending the University of Detroit Law School. Three years later, he graduated from the FBI Academy as a Special Agent and headed west.

In Seattle and Tacoma, Washington, he investigated a variety of crimes before being transferred to San Francisco where he tracked communist spies throughout Northern California.

Upon the collaspse of the Communist Party underground apparatus, he was transferred to FBI Headquarters where he subsequently directed the famed Ten Most Wanted Fugitives Program for thirteen years. Murderers, kidnappers, and bank robbers were his favorite fugitives to place on the "Top Ten" list. A believer in gender equality, he takes credit for adding the first woman to the list.

Returning to field investigations, he led the search for the first escapees from the "escape-proof" Federal Penitentiary at Marion, Illinois, built as a replacement for Alcatraz. After other challenging field assignments, he retired in Norfolk, Virginia, as Special Agent in Charge. He then spent ten years as Vice President of an international security firm in Washington, D.C., before settling in Virginia Beach and becoming active in civic, fraternal, community, church, and writing pursuits.

The proud father of six, he writes from his comfortable retreat on the Chesapeake Bay.

Made in the USA
Columbia, SC
12 January 2019